TRAPPED

SALLY BRYAN

Trapped

This book is a work of fiction. Events, situations, people and places are all products of the author's imagination. This book contains pornographic scenes and reader discretion is advised.

First Printing, 2014

ISBN-13: 978-1985606784

ISBN-10: 198560678X

CONTENTS

ANYONE BUT HER

The ball was blocked and then bumped. What's more, it now came my way, at a speed that should have been a simple spike and an easy point for New Forest Ladies. Only, for whatever reason, I'd never played such a poor game in all my volleyball playing days. Maybe it was because I was dehydrated, perhaps it had something to do with the measly two hours sleep I'd had the night before or maybe it could have been because Katelyn was back from injury and now sat on the bench waiting to take my place. Whatever the reason for my awful performance, if I didn't score this next point, Katelyn would most likely take my place for the rest of this crucial game. We were second in the league with only a few games left of the season and we needed to win.

The six opposing players were like blurs in my periphery vision. I was aware of their exact presence on the court without even having to look; a vital skill that had become a honed instinct over my five years playing the sport, a skill that enabled me to keep my eye on the ball as I prepared to spike it.

But then I was also aware of Katelyn perched on the bench, leaning forward, and my attention that should have been fully on the ball, wasn't.

Both teams were level; one game apiece and in this final deciding game, we were down by five points, mainly because of my prior mistakes. It was now or never. I had to spike this and score to allow us the chance of getting back into the match.

The pressure was on and the crowd gave a collective gasp, anticipating the point that could change everything; if not for the game then for me personally.

Katelyn, along with the rest of the bench watched as I sprang from the floor, fist clenched in readiness to strike the ball. Katelyn...

It was last year's end of season ball when it happened.

We'd finished second in the league, a record for us and so we were particularly happy to be celebrating. James and I had spent a fortune on our outfits as well as a photographer and limo to take us to the university for the big celebration. The ball itself was held on The Atrium under a giant marquee, a short walk from the gym where we trained. It seemed like everybody was there; players from a hundred sports and their partners, coaching staff, sponsors, league administrators and even a few celebrity sportsmen to hand out trophies.

Katelyn, who'd brought a female friend along, sat at the same table as James and myself. Several times I caught her making gooey eyes at him as we ate our calamari. I couldn't blame her, he looked truly dapper in his expertly cut tux which his torso and arms filled out impressively, his wavy blond hair framing his chiselled jaw and high cheekbones.

It was some time during the dancing when Katelyn's friend stormed out, causing Katelyn to run after her and a few minutes later, James excused himself to go to the bathroom. When he hadn't returned after twenty minutes, I went to look for him. One of the players on the men's team told me the bathroom was empty so, worried, I left the marquee in search of my boyfriend.

His cell went straight through to voicemail so I searched the foyer, car park and then the many corridors of the main university building. I arrived at the gym and thought it strange to find the lights on, despite all the players supposedly being at the ball. Not expecting to find him here, I pushed open the door anyway. It was a decision that was to change my life.

I froze - Two people were kissing on the benches.

"James?" I gasped as my cell fell from my grasp to clatter against the floor.

Wide eyed, he pulled away from Katelyn. He'd been sprung and there was nothing he could say or do.

Thinking about it in the days that followed, although I was deeply hurt, I couldn't blame him really. We'd only been together three months and although I was probably in love with him, I think, we'd never had sex. I just wasn't ready, the moment had never felt right and I wanted my first time to be special. So I guess he'd just tired of waiting and hearing endless excuses from me - Like I said, I couldn't blame him really.

Katelyn, however, had given him the kind of eyes that could not be interpreted any other way – That she wanted him! Added to that her long, slim, toned legs which were fully on display in that red dress, along with breasts that stretched out the thin fabric of the material, then I realise that any hot blooded male who was denied sex in his relationship would succumb to Katelyn's obvious charms. She looked briefly down as James

searched for something to say, but to my eyes it didn't seem like
it was out of embarrassment, as her long brown hair reflected
back the lights from above. Her athletic body, which had been
leaning toward him slowly straightened, composed, like nothing
was amiss with the overwhelming circumstances, her breasts
further pushing out as she did and her eyes fixing on mine from
across the gym. She crossed one leg over the other and for a beat
I thought I detected one side of her mouth slowly curling into a
smile, though in truth I could have been wrong about that.

My heart thumped agonisingly hard, my hands quivered.
Though it was strange how my first thought was not of
retaliation or any pitiful display of desperation in the face of
losing my boyfriend to a teammate. No, instead my mind went
into self-preservation mode. "You can have him!" And as soon as
I'd blurted it out, only then, for a flicker, did I think I detected a
hint of regret on Katelyn's face as she drew her head back with a
mouth slightly parted, though in truth, in such moments, a
hundred sensations are magnified and there's no telling what's
real and what's merely imagined and even now the whole event,
and my memories of it, are a weird haze.

Perhaps it was karma then that a few days later she
dislocated her shoulder spiking a volleyball in an after-season
friendly match. It meant I wouldn't be reminded of that awful
evening for a long time, by the mere sight of her face. But now
she was back and here she was...Katelyn.

She came into my line of sight as my fist launched to spike
the ball. But I felt no contact as my flailing hand moved through
empty air, the ball coming to bounce hopeless on our side of the
court. The referee blew her whistle, a point to the opposition.

"That was an easy one," Marie chastised me, "what
happened?"

"I'm sorry, I..."

...Dorothy called timeout and signalled for a substitution. She glanced at me and beckoned with an angry hand.

I knew who was replacing me, who else could it be? After all, we did both play as outside hitter but still, I prayed it wasn't her. "Please not the bitch." I muttered as I trudged off court.

Katelyn stood from the bench, her long tanned legs summoning a foray of wolf whistles from the crowd. She unzipped her New Forest Ladies jacket and threw it to the bench behind her. The motion exposed her arms and other assets, provoking an even louder cheer from the male spectators who watched from the bleachers. Her hair was tied back into a bun to reveal a graceful jaw, high cheekbones and a svelte neck. Maybe she'd dislocate her shoulder again, I could only hope.

I approached the bench, knowing full well my teammates would be excited to see how I was about to react. Shaking the hand of your replacement was the customary thing, not just in volleyball but in most team sports. Katelyn was leaning away and looked down to avoid my gaze as I neared and then with uncertainty, her arm half extended but there was no receiving hand to meet hers. Instead, I walked straight past and took my seat at the far end, consequently having to blank out the jeers from the spectators. That was the easy bit. Dealing with Dorothy, the team coach after the match for my unsporting behaviour would be the hard part. But rather that a hundred times than shake the bitch's hand.

Almost immediately, Katelyn made an impact on the match; scoring a point with her first touch and bringing the serve back to the home team. It was painful to watch - Several months out with injury had not diminished her skill, timing or sheer power, as she struck the ball home again. It was like watching a caged animal finally unleashed against its captors after months in captivity, being starved of food and prodded with a stick. After she won her fifth consecutive point, drawing the game level, the opposition began to panic, swearing at each other for missing the impossible lightning bolts that came shooting from Katelyn. On the tenth point, they called a timeout and it was then I noticed James far off to my side, several rows back, cheering his girl as she single-handedly turned the game around in our favour. He was euphoric, on his feet and his cheers cut through me like a rasping cough. Katelyn brought the game to fifteen points to five and the opposition made a substitution of their own, yet it made little difference. At twenty, the local news reporter rose to her feet and stood positioned in anticipation with her back to the court, camera facing her. Even the elderly principle of the university, who seldom came to watch us play, was punching the air about her.

Then Marie, the team setter, bumped the ball in Katelyn's direction for the final point. Katelyn watched as the ball arced toward her and crouched into a half squat in preparation for the jump, the musculature in her legs straining with the effort as she pushed off from the ground. She stretched her arm behind her head and threw her clenched fist forward, striking the ball with immense force. It shot down into the opposition court like a cannonball fired from some high up place at helpless soldiers below.

The referee blew the whistle as the New Forest Ladies ran to embrace their hero. The news reporter crowed into the microphone as excitement unfolded everywhere.

My volleyball future had been sealed. I was now surplus to requirements, my position on the team taken by the same girl who'd stolen my boyfriend.

THIRTY MINUTES LATER, ONCE THE ELATION OF SNATCHING victory from defeat had almost died down, we finally made it to the changing rooms. I had tried to look happy, to be a team player and join in on the celebrations, but I was never the kind of girl who was comfortable being false. I was certain my true feelings were etched upon my face and that they came to the fore as even now, Katelyn was being interviewed for the local news.

"Well done ladies." Dorothy said once everybody had settled down.

Our small changing room was particularly claustrophobic now that Katelyn had returned from injury. She was a tall girl, especially for an outside hitter but I wondered if it was the size of her ego that made the room appear even smaller, at least to my mind.

Dorothy beamed at her. "And I'd like to give a very special *well done* to our returning superstar, Katelyn." Oh, how I knew that was coming.

She blushed and her tanned skin turned a slight red. "Thanks, Coach, but I really couldn't have done it without Marie's passes."

Dorothy dismissed Katelyn's modesty with the flap of a hand. "Well, welcome back. Keep up that kind of performance and you'll be going to Rio with the national team." She shifted her gaze from her little superstar to me. "Jessica, when you're substituted, it's usual sporting behaviour to shake the hand of your replacement." She shook her head. "How you acted was completely unacceptable and if you do that again then I'll have no option but to suspend you from the team, at least until you learn proper conduct...And in front of the press too." It wasn't pleasant being singled out in front of my teammates, who for the most part were finding temporary interest in the changing room floor tiles, but considering everything, I now had to decide if I still wanted to think of them as my *teammates*. "You made a show of the whole team, Jessica, and if that little stunt makes it to the local paper, we won't look too good with the sponsors."

She left her words to hang in the air as the temperature increased and the air became almost stifling. I guessed I was supposed to use the silence to apologise, if not to the team then to Katelyn personally, but no way was I about to do that, no way, and instead I stared straight ahead defiant and expressionless, save for my jaw that clenched of its own accord.

Eventually Dorothy sighed and changed tone. "On a happier note, our team bonding ski trip to Italy is next week. It's been a long time coming ladies so I hope you've been getting in some practice down at the ski centre. Lord knows, but there are some of us here who could use some team bonding." Even though I guessed that was a dig at me, she spoke whilst looking at Katelyn.

I'd been looking forward to the ski trip for months and didn't think I'd be able to afford another holiday for at least two years. I'd also been regularly practising down at the local XScape, an indoor ski slope that blew snow from huge generators attached to the ceiling. I also knew that mercifully, due to Katelyn's absence and injury she had not been around to pay the funds to come on the trip, so I would probably consider this a farewell voyage with my teammates before retiring from volleyball forever.

Dorothy spoke almost as an afterthought, "and Katelyn, your

funds cleared this morning. I trust the injury didn't prevent you putting in some practice hours?"

"Not as much as I'd have liked, but I've been down a few times the last couple of weeks." Katelyn reassured everybody and Marie wrapped an arm around her shoulder in a gesture of comfort.

I was beginning to think Katelyn had just undergone the most miraculous return from any injury in history – But more to the point – She was coming on the bloody ski trip!

"Right, into the shower girls," Dorothy demanded, "I'd like all that filth and sweat removed this minute. We can't have the second in the league walking around stinking like this." She wafted the air in front of her face and headed for the exit.

I jumped up and ran out after her into the corridor. "Dorothy?"

She turned around with the kind of look an impatient mother gives her child. "Jessica?"

"It's not too late to pull out and get a refund is it? It's just that I'm not too sure skiing is really my thing." The one thousand pounds I'd scraped together could be better used on a holiday where I wouldn't be around Katelyn.

"You want to pull out? No Jessica, that won't be possible."

"Oh, I see."

She pursed her lips in defiance but then her resolve dissipated and her eyes softened.

"Actually I'm glad we're having this little chat. Look, Jessica, I'm fully aware of the problems between you and Katelyn..."

I felt my eyes involuntarily widen. Just how many people were aware of my private life?

"And it's unfortunate you both play the same position and that everything came to a head today. But you're a twenty year old woman and every now and then life will throw up these kinds of obstacles. You'll never grow as an individual if you avoid, duck and dive them your whole life."

"Yes, but I think this is a little different and..."

"...Well I don't. This is just one of those things you'll have to deal with, being an adult and everything." Although I thought she was being harsh, her wisdom could not easily be ignored. She was an excellent volleyball coach and also, as it turned out, she knew a thing or two about life. "I know you're not the kind of girl to ditch the team, Jessica, and besides, I believe that you and *Katelyn* in particular *need* this trip. You should both use the opportunity to settle your differences...for the good of the team."

"Um, yes."

She nodded once, as though that was final and she had a way of making you not want to cross or contradict her. "So I'll see you at the airport on Sunday." She said finally, turning around and stomping down the corridor, little knowing that the *good of the team* was no longer a factor in my thoughts.

I returned to the changing rooms where the steam from the showers was now filling the area where playing shorts and jerseys, socks and tennis shoes littered the benches. Water splashing against tiles and being sloshed about resonated throughout the room. I hated those showers. The university had failed to upgrade the group shower to individual cubicles and being the shy kind of girl, I always felt paranoid showering around so many women, even though they were my teammates. These women were athletes, with the type of sleek, honed bodies that went with being athletes. And even though I knew my body compared favourably to any of theirs, I was still totally self-conscious about it, about being naked around them. One thing that bothered me so much was that none of the other girls appeared to be introverted in the slightest. It was like showering around other girls was all natural to them, but not to me.

I stripped down but left my underwear in place. So I'd look an idiot, I didn't care. I crossed an arm over my breasts, as I always did, in a half-hearted attempt at concealing myself. This way, at least in my own head, it wouldn't look like I was deliberately trying to cover myself up. I'd noticed new players over the years doing similar things sans with the underwear, only, most girls usually lost their inhibitions within a few weeks, whereas I, after five years of playing the sport, still hadn't.

A narrow entry lay between the changing area and the shower and as I stepped into the threshold, Katelyn was coming the other way. Her dripping frame blocked my entrance and I had to step back to save from bumping into her. She was oblivious to my presence as her hands were stretched behind her head, squeezing water from her long brown hair, the slightest bulge of feminine biceps popping from her arms. It wasn't intentional, but in an effort to avoid making eye contact my gaze went to some other place, lowering and instead fixed over her breasts. It was only a split second, but in these confrontational moments I find my brain slows time down and heightens my senses. Maybe it's the masochist in me that made me stare, that made me want to compare, just so I could understand, why James had chosen her over me. And as, for a flash, her two large, perfectly symmetrical, firm breasts lay exposed to my eyes, I knew she was far superior to me in that area. No, I would not be consoling myself, and my ego, safe in the knowledge I was more a woman than she. I would not be smirking inwardly tonight, knowing James had made the decision few other men would have. It didn't help my fragile state of mind to see Katelyn as

James doubtless did, and to realise I was still in agony over the breakup, more so than I had previously thought and worse, I knew her womanly image would remain in my head as a painful reminder of what I wasn't.

Her foot scuffed on the tile and she looked up with a start. "Whoops, excuse me." She brought her arms back to her sides and exhibited no hint of nerves at being exposed, which I just couldn't relate to. I also realised it was the first thing either of us had spoken to the other since the horrific incident that started all this.

I avoided eye contact again as I stepped to the side, allowing her to pass as the faint scent of spearmint washed over me. Water dripped from her every curve and once again, I couldn't stop myself, even though I uselessly tried to fight it, I needed to know, and the masochist in me won as I turned my head in a futile attempt to understand.

Her buttocks were like marble and could have been sculpted by some master renaissance craftsmen, her skin tight and flawless as she strode away to vanish into the steam that enveloped my eyes.

I swallowed, breathed deeply and charged through the steam, throwing on the cold water and ensuring I remained there long enough for the bitch to leave.

THE THREE YEAR PHYSIOTHERAPY DEGREE I WAS TAKING AT Southampton University had a week long break at the end of January, which came as perfect timing for the ski trip. It was the final year of my degree and although I needed to study hard for the final exams in May, I was in the enviable position of already having completed most of my coursework. I was way ahead of the majority of my group and so could enjoy the forthcoming trip knowing I deserved a break.

Apart from studying, I also worked a few shifts every week at the local Starbucks. It was nice being able to get out of the house I shared with three other students and begin my journey up the ladder. I figured, if only working at a place that served coffee, I could prove to future employers I was a hard worker with people skills. Those skills would be transferrable to physiotherapy, where I hoped to start my career after graduating.

I'd recently been transferred to my present outlet from the Starbucks across town following an unfortunate incident with a regular customer who just couldn't take *no* for an answer. He had a habit of waiting until after I began my shift before entering and ordering his coffee and I used to wonder just where he was watching me from. Then he would frequently ask me out on dates. At first it was a harmless bit of fun until he became aggressive after being rejected. The time came that as soon as he entered, I would go on my break just to avoid him. I was told by a colleague that he would ask for my address when I wasn't there. After that, it was decided the best thing would be for me to transfer. Of course, I occasionally had guys asking me out on dates, and once or twice even had flowers bought for me, but seldom did I ever experience a borderline stalker.

"How're you finding things? You're ok with the Mastrena?" Kieron asked, referring to the coffee machine we used.

I released a jet of air from the milk steamer to clean the spout. "Of course, we used the same machine over at the West Quay store."

He placed a hand on my shoulder, a gesture I wasn't quite expecting, and I could feel the moisture through my blouse.

"Well if there's anything you're not sure about or anything you're finding different, just give us a shout."

Kieron was the store manager, who'd picked up the nickname 'Tiny' on account of having the need to duck every time he entered a room, though the touchy feely kind of familiarity I hadn't yet achieved with the guy, at least from my perspective. I noticed how he treated me different to the others; how he was managerial with the rest, yet with me, he always seemed to be looking for my approval. It was the way he'd crack jokes, then look with hopeful eyes to see if I found them funny. He also talked a lot about the money he makes in stocks and shares, like it was presumed I'd find his business acumen impressive.

I occupied myself by wiping the spout with a cloth as I spoke, being as polite as possible. "Thank you, Kieron, I'll remember that."

After half a minute I sensed his presence still lingering close by and checked the reflection in the coffee machine's metallics to see him leaning casually back against the countertop, still facing me from behind. "Just thought I'd let you know I made another thousand quid this month on the market...a little over perhaps...should prob do even better next month the way that new startup's going."

I quietly sighed, lamented it was so quiet today and turned to face him, grabbing a tray. "Excuse me, looks like it's my turn to do the rounds." I approached the seating area where used cups and plates, crumbs and napkins lay strewn over the empty tables, so I cleared them away and gave each surface a wipe. I didn't mind this kind of work as it was therapeutic and gave my mind time to think. It was often whilst cleaning tables I could ponder my present situation in life. The only downside now was that

Katelyn, for whatever reason, came to the fore. Despite any recent relapses, understandably brought on by the feeling of being crushed after losing my position on the team, she really had done me a great favour, by taking James away. I had not been in love with the guy, well not really, and if anybody was about to steal him from me then it was far better it happened before I developed those kinds of feelings than afterwards when the consequences would have been far worse. No, Katelyn had done me a good turn and it was all for the best, of that I was certain and besides, my self-confidence would soon recover just as soon as I achieved a first in physiotherapy, found a new team and a new man, I knew, as I brushed a piece of squashed muffin from my apron. So then why was I still angry about the whole incident of months gone by, and why did I, even now, hate Katelyn so much? I didn't like carrying around so much hatred and figured it was because it just so happened to be the same bitch who'd taken *both* James and my position as outside hitter. Thinking about it logically, on balance Katelyn had been good for me - So then why did I still want to scratch her eyes out? None of it made any sense.

I finished cleaning the ground floor and walked upstairs. As always, it was half filled with students, some of whom I recognised as they busied themselves with laptops. I made my way around the corner into the sofa area and noticed two pairs of feet pull inwards as I squeezed by to access the large table in the centre.

"Jessica?" Came the voice.

I looked up and gasped. It was *them*.

They were just as surprised to see me as I was them; James and Katelyn were sitting snuggly together, his arm draped over her shoulder as she leaned back into him. Her eyes widened as did his, my heart thumped, I did not need this right now, or ever.

"Oh, hello." I said, wanting to blank them out but wavering between that and the need to remain professional to customers, so instead I averted my eyes to scrutinise the heap of rubbish and spills they'd kindly left for me to clean.

"Jessica, I'm sorry, I thought you worked at the other Starbucks." James squeaked, readjusting himself and causing an audible ripple of leather couch. Well, at least he admitted to be actively avoiding me, which was kind of considerate.

"Not anymore, I work here now." It wasn't comfortable for me either and my palms were sweating as I seized cups and plates from the table, what a mess. I plucked up a sachet of sugar and cursed as the brown Demerara fanned out over the surface. My forehead itched as I stooped down to scoop up the mess, my eyes flicking once over them, their eyes full of pity, James readjusting his collar, the bitch fidgeting with a napkin, my chest constricting.

"Well, I hope you're having a nice weekend." James almost whimpered, taking his arm away from around Katelyn's shoulders, doubtless to make the situation just a tiny bit less awkward and brushed the hair away from his eyes.

My forehead burned and for a second I wondered if a bead of sweat had dropped to the table top.

"Excuse me, love?" A middle-aged man's voice boomed from the next couch. "Excuse me, love?" He cried again and I looked up with raised eyebrows. "You can take this coffee away, love, it went cold. You're supposed to heat the cups to stop that happening, or so I thought."

"I'm sorry, let me take that from you." I reached over the table, aware my backside was pointing in Katelyn's face and moved for the cup. Only, my hand-eye coordination hadn't improved much from last night's volleyball match and my fingers clattered into the side of the mug, knocking it into the man's lap.

He leapt up, coffee stains down the length of his leg. "Shit, and I only bought these last week." Though his voice was calm and measured, probably due to his female company, he still loomed over me in a threatening posture.

The temperature rose to some unbearable level. "I'm so sorry, let me get something to help you clean up."

I ran downstairs, mind a blur and found my colleague Jenny, who thankfully wasn't too busy. "Please help me, I spilled coffee over a guy upstairs and don't think I can face him again. I'd be so grateful if you could take up some stain remover and pacify the guy?"

"Ok, but you owe me one." She smiled, reached to the side of the cash register and brought out a few bits of paper. "You know, we have vouchers we usually give out when these things happen." Now that was one thing we didn't do at the West Quay Starbucks.

The heat, my underarms feeling damp, lightheadedness and now a queasiness in my belly. I needed to sit down with a glass of cold water and so I pottered over to Kieron and asked if I could go on an early break.

He looked at his watch and his forehead creased, "sure, go ahead," he agreed after a short hesitation.

I knew I was taking advantage and also leaving Kieron on his own, but I'd never had such an awkward experience in all my life and sometimes sanity has to come first.

I went downstairs into the staff room, shut the door, turned off half the lighting and collapsed on the couch with a glass of water. I began concentrating on taking deep breaths and within a couple of minutes my composure began to seep back.

What had just happened? Was it James who'd had that effect on me or was it Katelyn? Or was it seeing them both together, arm in arm with no warning? I could be forgiven for panicking and losing it, it was just unfortunate *they* had to witness it. But I was beginning to think going on a skiing trip where *that* girl would be around me the whole time was not something that would be beneficial to my present state of mind. Whether intentional or not, she had the ability to turn me into an extremely negative person simply by virtue of her mere presence. I dreaded to think what I'd become if I had to spend an entire week around her person, even if others were there to dilute it.

No – The best thing to do on Sunday, rather than go to the airport, would instead be to head to the library for an extended study session followed by the pool for a swim. Sure, I'd lose the money I paid but there were far more important things in life. I was much more concerned with the prospect of not having a final time away with the girls, but I'd be sure to keep in touch with them after leaving the team.

So, that was final - No ski trip for me. And as soon as I'd made the deliberation, I felt better for it.

The door creaked open and Kieron entered, bobbing his head beneath the frame as he did. He said nothing as he opened the fridge, delved somewhere to the back and pulled out a Tupperware filled with something that glowed green through the plastic, salad perhaps? He then forewent the table in the room's centre and even the other two couches, instead choosing to squeeze himself into the small gap beside me. In no way was the couch big enough for two, especially when one of those was bordering on being seven feet tall and I had no room to shuffle away. Oh, he carried a presence, that was for sure, but my thoughts soon turned to just who was taking care of things upstairs, considering the Saturday lunch stampede would soon be coming. Poor Jenny would be struggling on her own and I did owe her a favour.

"How you feeling? You looked a little flushed earlier." Kieron asked all concern, stretching out his pins and turning to face me.

"Oh thank you, yes, I met an old friend and guess I got a little emotional. Sorry." I downed the water and prepared to head back up. "I'm just about done here so I'll leave you to enjoy your lunch."

"Hang on just a second, Jess." He peeled off the container lid to reveal not salad, but what I could only assume to be some chicken or fish concoction, it really was impossible to tell. The bright green colour was either mould or fungus but it was the unbearable smell that accompanied its release that made me want to bolt for the door. I wouldn't ask how long it'd been in the fridge sharing living space with everybody else's food.

I held my breath and stood. "Yes, Kieron?"

"I was thinking of heading out for a couple of drinks after work, you know, just to Oasis, if you fancied coming along?" He awaited my answer and shovelled some green substance in his mouth in a fine attempt at appearing aloof.

What did I have to do to find a job where I wouldn't have to deal with being hit on? And by my boss now. I wasn't daft and knew where this was heading but neither did I have the desire to be in a toxic working environment from giving an answer he wouldn't like, so I decided to play it naive.

"Sounds fun, Kieron. Is Jenny coming too? It'd be nice to get to know her a little better...seems like a friendly girl."

He squinted. "Jenny? Yeah, she's alright. But call me Tiny... It's kind of an ironic thing I've had most of my life." He laughed and I prayed he was referring to his height.

I kept my face serious. "So she's coming then?"

He shuffled and the leather creaked. "Well no, not exactly. I thought it'd be a nice chance for the two of us to get to know each other a little better."

I unconsciously stepped closer to the door, more to get away from the smell of whatever it was he was eating than from an automatic reaction to getting hit on by a guy I wasn't in the least attracted to. It's true that I wasn't expecting this, but I still hoped to control my body language enough so as not to appear rude.

"Oh, I see." I tried to appear as surprised as I could and brought a hand to my chest. "That's kind of you, Tiny, and I'm flattered, but I'm too recently out of a big relationship and I don't think I'm ready for that kind of thing right now. I'm kind of just keeping my head down and getting on with things at the moment. In fact, the *old friend* I mentioned before was kind of my ex and I'm really not ready for anything else right now. But thanks, really." It came out almost as a babble but as gentle as I could make it. Now please, please, please accept the rejection with decency. I motioned with a hand limply to the door as I thought more and more about returning to work as fast as possible.

And then he dropped the bomb. "Well, who said anything about *relationship*? I just thought it'd be nice for the two of us to get to know each other a little better. No harm in that, Jess." He shovelled in another mouthful of his toxic meal. "Can't two adults go out for a few drinks without things getting complicated?"

Oh classy – At this rate I'd soon need another transfer. "Look, Tiny, I hope I didn't give the wrong impression? If I did then I'm sorry. But I'm not the kind of girl who goes to bars often anyway. But I'm flattered. Can we leave it at that please?"

He was a harmless guy, but far too often men just didn't get the message. If I'm friendly and listen to their stories of stock exchange glory then it doesn't necessarily mean I'm interested in them.

"Oh, ok." Tiny said, his face giving away his disappointment, and now *I* felt like the bad guy. "Well, if you change your mind..."

"Thanks for your understanding." I left the room and ran upstairs.

Would coming to work be awkward in future? I now understood why people had personal policies against dating work colleagues.

Back on the shop floor, I found Jenny in a near state of panic; taking orders and making drinks all on her own. The queue stretched out the door and along the store front window and several customers now tut-tutted as I appeared. It would seem Tiny had abandoned his duties to take his chances with me, and he was the guy supposedly in charge around here.

Jenny saw me, her reddened face giving way to a smile. "Jess, thank God."

Getting away from everything, from work and Tiny to go skiing now seemed more appealing; if only for a week, things would be less awkward around this place when I returned. But on balance, I still knew I did not want to be around that bitch, even for a second, which truly was saying something that still, I'd rather be here than on a beautiful Italian mountainside.

No – Skiing was off the table.

CRUSH

*T*he student house was a mess, as per usual. Noise from a football game blaring from the TV in the living room resounded around the entire ground floor.

I pushed open the door and scrutinised the scene of my housemates vibrating on the couch, immersed fully in the game. Beer bottles lay about in a liberal fashion, the smell of ale filling the room. It was several seconds before anybody noticed me standing there.

"Jess!" Ben yelled, holding his Bud up to me in a gesture of *cheers*. The fact I had no bottle of my own in which to return the gesture escaped him.

"Hi honey. Are you joining us?" Elli asked from her seated position next to Ben.

After meeting Ben and Elli on my course, it didn't take long for the three of us to become great friends. But it was only after we started renting our accommodation together that they began dating. I was happy for them and their relationship was wonderful. Together, they made up two of my three housemates, which only left...

"Hi Jess, you're looking nice." Chris said between sips of beer. I was in my Starbucks outfit so wasn't sure how nice I could possibly look.

Chris was also enrolled on the same physiotherapy course as the rest of us. As well as that he played Rugby and despite the huge competition for places, he'd made it into the New Forest University team, competing nationally against other universities. He knew exactly what he wanted in life and that was to be a physiotherapist for a top rugby team. Like the rest of us in the house, Chris was an athlete and he certainly looked it too. His muscular frame commanded the attention of most rooms, the ladies especially drooled over him and with the arrangement already existing in the house, with two of our occupants already dating, everyone else just assumed it was logical that the two of us would get together at some point. Ben and Elli had on many occasions joked about it but more recently, due to my being single, the jokes had turned into borderline peer pressure, which thus far I'd managed to humour.

"When are you and Chris gonna start dating, Jess? It would be so perfect with the four of us." Elli said the other week. "It's your fault we can't go on cheaper holidays." She remarked more recently.

Of course, none of this banter, because that's all it was, even mattered because as of yet, Chris himself had not once demonstrated even one single flicker of interest, no drunken slips, no eye contact lingering across the room, nothing, nada. So I was content to allow my other two meddling housemates to continue in their amateur matchmaking because it was all in good fun and kept them entertained.

"I'm making pasta salad if anyone's hungry?" I asked aloud to goggling eyeballs on the screen.

"Nah, we're off out soon. We're gonna grab a few drinks but you're welcome to come if you'd like?" Ben asked.

"That's nice of you, but I think I'll just go sit in my room and study. Have fun though."

I took the meal upstairs and ate whilst studying in my desk's lamp light. Not exactly the best Saturday night in the world, but I was never one for drinking myself into a stupor and besides, after the day I'd had, I just wanted an early night.

It wasn't for an hour until I received a knock on the door.

"Come in." I called, averting my eyes from the textbook. "Hey, I thought you lot were gone for the night?"

Chris pottered in and half closed the door behind him. "Yeah, we were, but I came home early." He was a big guy with lots of confidence, which made him even more attractive, although right now, you wouldn't know it. "You, uh, don't have a copy of Orthopaedic Physical Assessment do you?" It came out higher pitched than usual as he fidgeted with his hands clasped before his belly.

"Hmm, actually I think I do." I scanned through the stack of books on my desk until I came to a thick one near the bottom. I levered it out and handed it to Chris. "It's not due back for a while so you can take your time with that one."

"Thanks, Jess." He half turned to leave but then looked back to me.

"You ok? Too excited to get stuck into the book on a Saturday night, huh? If you have problems with the big words then bring it back and maybe I can help you out."

He laughed nervously, scratched the back of his neck and

perched on the edge of my desk. "You see, Jess, it's reasons like this..."

"Reasons like what?"

He hesitated then spoke still fidgeting. "You make me laugh."

"Well good, but your fat arse is blocking my light."

This time he didn't laugh and seemed to be focusing hard on me, serious, and he took a deep breath. "Jess, I'm not sure I can carry on like this any longer." And then he placed his hand on mine and my eyes widened and I felt something cold stir in my belly.

I glared at his hand then looked away, wanting to hide, momentarily lost for words, startled. Where did *that* come from? "Um, Chris?"

"Jess, I..."

Oh God.

"...Jess, I like you. I actually *really* like you and have for a long time." He finally managed to blurt out.

I didn't know how to react to this revelation and all I could do was sit frozen like an idiot. I mean, I had no idea he felt that way. "What? Why? Since when?"

He stood and strode to the wall, running a hand through his hair. "I don't know, probably since about the time I first saw you." His leg was visibly shaking now. "You're just so beautiful and I can't stand it any longer."

I exhaled an involuntary breath. "You must be blind, Chris, I'm definitely not beautiful. My boyfriend left me for another girl remember. It doesn't exactly do wonders for one's confidence."

"Yeah, well he was a stupid little bastard and you're better off without him." He declared with one hand balled into a fist.

"Well, I would agree with you there."

"And I hated seeing you with him, I mean, *really* hated it. I should have been angry after what he did to you, but the truth is I wasn't." He now took my hand in both of his. "No, instead I was ecstatic because *I* want you."

I didn't know what to think. This was all hitting so fast that my fingers were tingling. Despite the jokes, I'd never even considered the possibility of a relationship with Chris; I guess we just never had that kind of chemistry. But more to the point - I certainly hadn't been *ecstatic* at the time. It was the single hardest period of my life, in fact I still wasn't completely over it, but here was my housemate, one of my friends feeling secretly happy all along. I guess his reasons were understandable, but that didn't mean I liked them.

I slipped my hand out from his grasp and rolled back on my chair's wheels. "You want me? I'm not a piece of meat you know."

"I know, sorry. But enough time's past by though hasn't it? I mean, you're over it all now, aren't you?"

I hesitated. "I think I am, yes, mostly, but I still have my moments of regression."

"Well, maybe if we got together then things would get easier." He was serious, which was almost funny, in a tragic way.

"It's not as simple as that, Chris, I'm not the kind of girl who jumps into a new relationship just because I'm over the last one and besides, where the heck did all this come from? I have to like a guy too you know."

He stepped closer and it was then, in the lamplight, that I saw the tears streaming down his face. "Jess, please. We could be *so* good together."

I stood, kicked the chair back on its wheels and it struck

hard against the bed. "Chris, this is all completely out of the blue. I'm going to say *no*, but thank you."

He took a single step toward me and I could smell the alcohol on his breath. Was I so terrifying that he dared not do this sober? Then his hands moved forwards and his fingers were in my hair. "Please." He pleaded.

Awkward much?

I jumped back, risked losing my hair in the process and pointed at the door. "Chris, now you're begging and quite honestly you're better than that."

His head dropped and he sniffed. "Yes, of course. I'm sorry." And finally, he stumbled out and I bolted the door after him.

Ugh, enough study for one night, the whole day needed writing off.

Thanks to Tiny the environment would be toxic at work and now because of Chris, life at home would be even more awkward. And to think that tomorrow my friends were all headed to Italy for a week of ski, fun, fine food and most of all, escapism.

I could use some of that now more than ever.

My suitcase stared down from atop the wardrobe, taunting me, begging me.

I yanked it down and began packing.

CORTINA D'AMPEZZO

I woke early to shower, have breakfast and ensure I packed as many guilty pleasures that could squeeze into my luggage. My weakness happened to be SoupInACup, strange I know, but they were typical student fare, and though I knew I'd be drinking Italian coffee and wine, I couldn't survive a whole week in the snow without my beloved SoupInACup. On a normal day I'd vanquish two or three sachets and although they didn't hold a great deal of nutrition, they were quick, easy, tasty and had thus far seen me through university.

Several of the girls were on the same train to Southampton Central and from there we met with the rest of the gang for the journey to Gatwick Airport. Luckily Katelyn was not on the train and I assumed James must have been driving her all the way to Gatwick, doubtless to spend extra precious minutes with her, not that I cared, really. But I was under no denial that I'd be crossing her path at some point, it was inevitable. When that moment arrived, I would endeavour to cling to Marie, who was probably my best friend on the whole team.

"You'll have to see her ugly face at some point," she panted as we rolled our luggage over the Gatwick tarmac, "and my guess is that time will soon arrive."

"Don't I know it." The feeling of impending dread had been building gradually since breakfast, which had now reached the point there was a knot in my belly.

As it happened, Katelyn was indeed dropped off by James. The entire group stood and stared through the large glass wall as the couple hugged each other in the area where taxis dropped off passengers. At least one teammate hummed with approval as though a couple hugging their goodbyes was so sweet. I'd have been in agreement if only it weren't those two. But for the most part, and thanks to the gossip, my friends were aware of the situation and tactfully turned away from it to look at the floor instead.

Marie caught my eye and rubbed my arm. "It's ok." She said forlornly as mucus built in my throat.

And then a terrible feeling struck me, which I knew was my being paranoid, but it was still there - What if the girls were only being tactful because they were expecting everything to blow up at some point? I ground my teeth as my right eye began to sting - Damn it, but I would not give anyone, least of all the bitch, the satisfaction of seeing me lose it this week.

But then as Katelyn approached, a general discomfort washed over the group and I was pretty sure it wasn't my imagination. Amanda scratched her head and Marie showed Katelyn her back, turning around with a sudden interest in the flight departure screen. I followed her lead and struck up a conversation about Italian men, which mercifully, made her face light up. Then with impeccable timing, Dorothy appeared from the direction of check-in and commenced chastising the group for not having already checked in our bags.

After a three hour plane journey we arrived at Venezia Marco Polo Airport. I'd always wanted to visit Venice, but unfortunately, the airport was not actually on the island of Venice itself, but on the Italian mainland. That trip would have to wait for another day.

We took a pre-rented minibus from the airport, which Dorothy's husband, Stewart drove. He was a big, chubby guy with a permanent smile and seemed happy to allow his wife to take charge and do her thing. I made certain to sit with Marie at the back of the minibus and we chatted about our previous skiing experiences while enjoying the Italian countryside. As it turned out, neither of us had ever been skiing outside of an indoor practice run in an English entertainment park.

I remained aware of where Katelyn polluted the bus with her presence, only two rows in front beside Amanda, the team's middle blocker. I'd so far managed to avoid the moment I knew would soon come, and unfortunately the longer that moment was delayed, the harder it would be.

Then Katelyn stood, slid out from her seat and stepped down the aisle, holding onto each headrest for stability as she went before stopping next to Dorothy and leaning in close to discuss something sotto voce. Then, oddly, Dorothy sat forward and craned her head to stare into the back of the bus, made brief eye contact with me, gave away nothing and turned back.

What the heck was that? It was most certainly one of those strange moments when you feel your ears burning. What were they talking about? Were they discussing me, conspiring, or had Katelyn finally succeeded in turning me into a paranoid ex volleyball player? Like taking my boyfriend and position on the team weren't enough, she now wanted my sanity too. Oh, it was sure hard to enjoy a nice journey through beautiful mountains with so much crap flying through the air.

After a couple more hours on the road, Dorothy stood and grabbed ahold of the post behind her seat. "All right girls, listen up." She boomed over the noise of the rickety old thing her husband was driving. "We're about thirty miles from Cortina so you'll begin to see a gradual increase in snow. Stewart will need his full concentration for the roads, so please could you all keep your loud chatter and occasional yelping to a quantity of decibels more pertaining to a group of ladies."

It was reasons like that, Dorothy's dry sense of humour, that made her such a hit with us. She wasn't subtle, quite the opposite in fact, and possessed great wit with an indefinable something that served not to alienate her from people. And then with impeccable timing, as she spoke, it did indeed begin to snow. The snow was also accompanied by a heavy gust that slammed against the side of the vehicle and I saw shoulders brace as some of the girls grabbed ahold of their seats.

"I have a few announcements to make so please listen carefully." She squinted into a piece of she held. "I'll need your passports, so for those of you who haven't yet handed them in, please remember to give them to me when we arrive. No passport, no accommodation. I have the bunking plan; girls, you must remember that if any of you happen to slink off with one of the locals, then you absolutely must tell your bunking buddy."

We all laughed at that and I heard someone repeat the word *bunking buddy* in good humour.

"Amanda's bunking buddy better be extra vigilant." Marie shouted and the whole minibus erupted into yet more laughter.

"All right, settle down." Dorothy chastised. "This is serious. Girls, look after your buddy, stick together, don't get lost and above all, have fun together. Now, here are the bunking arrangements; Marie will be with Amanda, which serves you right...Tina and Holly are together, Sally and Kelly will be bunking buddies, Victoria and Grace," she glanced at me and I immediately knew where this was going, "Jessica, that means you'll be bunking with Katelyn and I trust there'll be no problems. Now, if we want to head for dinner after we arrive then you'll have to be quick. Check in, go to your cabins, dump your bags and come straight back to the bus. The town itself is a short drive from where we're staying and I'm sure you're all starving, so let's make it quick."

She continued to speak, whilst I glared at her with cold eyes, mainly about renting out ski equipment the next day but most of that information went straight through my head. We were all booked to stay in ski cabins, each of which accommodated two people. The prospect of being all cozied up with Katelyn was not something I looked forward to and for the first time today, I regretted my decision to come on the trip, not that there was anything I could do about it now. No, they'd done this deliberately, the pair of them, it was so obvious. Did they really think that forcing me to bunk up with *that* girl for seven nights would mean that by the end of it we'd be best friends and all would be forgiven? How ridiculous. It was just fortunate I'd happened to pack a physiotherapy textbook and headphones so I could justifiably ignore the girl, so if Dorothy and the usurper thought I'd meekly take this, they were wrong. Though why on earth Katelyn wanted and had even manipulated the bunking arrangements to be around me I just couldn't fathom. Perhaps she got off on my misery and insecurities, there were stranger people out there, that was for sure.

The Dolomite Mountains were stunning, even if I did have to stare into the back of Katelyn's scheming head, and for a long while the minibus went up and up and up. Stewart drove extra carefully on the roads as they became gradually more hazardous and the snow became thicker and thicker. However, the roads were in great condition and were obviously ploughed at regular intervals.

A short time later the minibus pulled into Mortisa, a tiny resort consisting of five holiday villas and ten ski cabins. Mortisa lay on a steep slope a little over a mile from the centre of Cortina d'Ampezzo. The two were joined by a narrow, unmade road with a thick blanket of trees on either side. In the last of the day's light it looked like we were heading into the abyss but I suppose that was half the thrill of the location.

Stewart pulled into the small gravel car park and we exited the vehicle. At once I was hit by the cold and a number of girls pulled on their gloves. The snow fell heavy but it was the strong wind and accompanying chill that made standing around uncomfortable.

Still, I stretched out my legs and examined the fine sight of our resort. It was a special place, that much was certain. If Cortina d'Ampezzo was surrounded by mountains on all sides, then Mortisa *was* one of those mountain slopes. Trees lay sporadically up the verge with the occasional large rock protruding from the surface. Other than that it was pure whiteness until the slope hit an enormous cliff top that looked to be miles in the distance. I had envisioned there being ski lifts though none were visible here. The real action, I assumed, must take place on the other side of the town. In actual fact, Mortisa was quite isolated, perhaps an extra factor that made our villas so extortionate to rent; on second glance they were extremely beautiful on the exterior and I hoped the inside was likewise. There was no denying Mortisa was an upmarket resort. It was just a pity about being inflicted with that boyfriend stealing bitch.

Dorothy returned from one of the villas with a padded envelope from which she removed several sets of keys and handed them out to the various groups of buddies. "Remember to be quick girls." She hunched her shoulders against the snow and grimaced when a flake found its way down her back.

I hung back by the minibus and allowed Katelyn to collect the keys. I didn't fancy coming over as being overly enthusiastic about this contrived little arrangement. As Dorothy handed over the keys, she gave me a look as if to say *I'm keeping an eye on you both*.

Then, with a shy grin, Katelyn jingled the keys in my face before trudging toward the cabin a short walk away. The other girls had all dispersed and I set off toward cabin 4 a couple of paces behind and to Katelyn's side. She carried an enormous backpack over one shoulder, typical of what you'd expect to find on a gap year traveller. Meanwhile I pulled along a wheelie bag that rattled as it trundled through the thickening snow. She didn't walk with her usual swagger, her shoulders remaining quite still, her big nose pointing downwards, and I wondered if it was due to the weight of her bag or a natural apprehensive reaction to being anxious in my company. Anxious, nervous and worried; she'd better be all those things and more. Those emotions I'd been through myself recently, but right now, I decided to be as aloof and uncaring as possible. I wouldn't give her the satisfaction of seeing me upset or beat up over this pathetic situation she'd engineered for her own sick ends.

The cabins were small from the outside with wooden exteriors and for whatever reason they made me imagine lumberjacks chopping wood whilst living self-sufficient lifestyles in the forest. There were times such a life appealed to me. Each cabin was separated from the next by large communal areas which, beneath the snow would doubtless be grass. The cabins would make ideal escapes during the summer months for when people wanted isolation and not skiing, however, right now, there'd be no escape for me.

Katelyn fumbled with the lock until finally she managed to open the door. She then felt around the inside wall for a light switch, pressed it and the inside illuminated. She half looked over her shoulder to check I was still present, that's how quiet I was being, and then dragged her lumbering form within.

I counted to five, exhaled a futile breath and trod in behind.

My first impression was that the interior walls were not wooden but stone. Two huge wooden pillars on which hung framed pictures of the town propped up the low arched roof. The roof was one of those beautiful wood supported structures you just don't get very often. A TV rested upon a table by one of the pillars and a small kitchen area was located in one corner of the room. Then it hit me. Because the cabin was almost completely open plan, all except for the bathroom, which would make escaping Katelyn's efforts of mending bridges all the harder to achieve. Worse still, the two double beds were located in the far corner of the cabin with only a small gap between them, meaning that even in my sleep there'd be no escape.

"Ooh, a fireplace." Katelyn headed toward the open fire that was set into the far wall opposite the entrance. A small pile of logs were stacked neatly to the side. "So cosy." She dropped her bag close to the hearth and I watched as she appraised the area, her hands on hips. Then she turned around and was immediately struck by the fact I'd been glaring into the back of her head with an expression you could use to cut the bloody kindling. You made this happen – Deal with it bitch!

"Are you ok, honey?" Katelyn asked, only making eye contact for half the question.

"Oh, sure." My expression remained fixed and I took a small matter of satisfaction in having stared her down.

Her mouth gaped once before she managed to speak as though nothing was amiss. "Well then, I guess we'd better head back to the bus. I'm sure you're really hungry and..."

I don't know why I did it, maybe it was the sound of her voice grating inside my head, but my plan to remain distant with the bitch turned immediately to shit, "...You arranged this with Dorothy, didn't you? I saw you do it...Stupid cow! That's how to ruin my trip...Not content with stealing my boyfriend, are you? And you weren't even supposed to be here."

By the look on her face; from the opened mouth to the dopey glazed over eyes, she had not been expecting that barrage. "Jess, I'm sorry, yes I did." She finally began with her palms wavering in some placatory gesture. "I can't stand having all this animosity between us. I really respect you as a person and a teammate and it doesn't do the team any good having two of its players at each other's throats. What I did with Dorothy I thought was for the best and..."

"...Oh shut up!" I cut the tramp off mid-flow with another angry expression before turning my back and heading for the team, and salvation, who were gathered by the bus, calling over my shoulder. "Just don't talk to me, bitch."

FINDING THE RIGHT WORDS TO DESCRIBE A SNOW COVERED Cortina d'Ampezzo in the dusk wasn't easy. It was magical, a fairyland and like something from a dream. The tourists who strolled the streets, even in the cold, added somewhat to the special atmosphere; it was a happy place and I certainly felt my mood lift.

For such a small town there were a wealth of restaurants. We wanted our first night in Italy to be special, so we had already agreed that we'd splurge for dinner on this night and then live more within our means the rest of the week. The problem came when trying to agree upon a restaurant to eat in. It was impressive, for Cortina d'Ampezzo had not just one Michelin starred restaurant, but two. In fact the Rosa Alpina had a double star, which settled the argument, and it was lucky we entered just as the wind picked up, blowing thick blankets of snow from the ground to mix with the snow that fell heavy from the sky.

Our group consisted of twelve people and were seated at a large table by the window overlooking the rear of the hotel. From my seat next to Marie, as far from Katelyn as I could get, I had a view of the swimming pool that verged right into dense forest. It was odd seeing the two things adjacent. What I hadn't bargained on, with the table being round, was that in endeavouring to get as far as possible from any particular person meant that I would inevitably end up positioned directly opposite them. The end result was that within the first minute of being seated, Katelyn and I had made eye contact no fewer than three times. The shimmering candlelight served to make her skin appear flawless and with her long brown hair let down and flowing over her shoulders, she looked beautiful even though she'd dressed for the weather, along with most of the rest of us, in New Forest Ladies team jersey over a hoody, which wasn't easy for me to admit. Indeed, it rubbed salt into my wound that was still trying so hard to heal and all I could do was hope the cold weather would make her skin break out.

Despite everything in the build up to this trip, not to mention the more recent contrivance, I was still ecstatic at the thought of testing out my skiing skills on some real runs and not the indoor kind with machine generated snow. There was electricity around the group, the kind that could only be created from excitement and even Dorothy appeared to vibrate in her seat as she told jokes in a voice even louder than usual.

The waiter appeared with the widest grin I'd ever seen. He'd sure struck lucky tonight with a table full of volleyball players and one of those players, Amanda, straightened in her seat at the first sight of 'Marco.' She was sure gifted with a fine pair of breasts, which she now pushed out as the waiter took her order. She also twirled a clump of hair around in her fingers, though whether or not she was aware of how obvious she was making her attraction look, I couldn't be sure.

"Hey, Jess, what do you think of him?" Marie asked, elbowing me a little too hard in the side.

"Ouch, Marie, I think I've had more than enough of men for the time being."

As the waiter made his way around the table, he caught sight of Katelyn and I definitely noticed his eyes widen and linger. Ok, so she was beautiful, but why did men have to be so perverted all the time? All I could think was that if our waiter friend had a girlfriend then she'd better be extra vigilant whilst Katelyn was in town. Let's face it, the usurper had a history of stealing men.

The wine arrived and it became immediately clear there were

many on the table who were hardly concerned about the prospect of being hungover for tomorrow's physical activity. But the girls were happy, which was infectious. The conversation degenerated from volleyball, of our upcoming games and hopes for winning the league this season, to comparing English men to Italian men, before degrading yet further, to a topic I dared not repeat, but which involved making certain comparisons, that may, or may not be substantiated. Oh, I was under no delusions as to the instigator of such wanton smut and depravity at the dinner table and it was lucky we sat by the window, with a fair distance between the more respectable diners and Marie, as much as I adored her.

Two waiters arrived with plates spread down the entire length of their arms. Accomplishing that with no spills must have been an acquired skill. The starters all looked like works of art, tiny specks of perfection on huge plates. I went for the 'Carpaccio Of Milk Fed Calf With Marinated Root Vegetables.' The flavour from each individual vegetable hit my palate like a firework. One of the girls made a big deal of Stewart's plate, which consisted of 'Snails In The Garden' – Not quite for me.

Dorothy was reading from her phone with an ever increasing grin. "Girls, I have some news." She ended up having to stand to gain the table's attention. "I've just received a text from Allison Burbridge."

The mere mention of the national team coach silenced us. I had a feeling I knew what was coming, as did a few of the other girls, who were now increasingly glancing over at Katelyn. Certainly, Dorothy was now looking straight at her.

She continued, "Allison will be attending next week's game against Worthing VC." A cheer erupted and the girls either side of Katelyn embraced her. "Girls, she made no mention of any particular reason for her visit or any player especially, so just remember it's a team effort, ok?"

Who was she kidding? We all knew Allison Burbridge was coming to watch Katelyn destroy Worthing VC practically solo and I had no doubt Katelyn *would* destroy them. I would never again push my way back into the squad, not in place of a national team player. If Katelyn took good care of her shoulder, she'd be going to Rio for the 2016 Olympics. As for me, if I couldn't find a new local team of the standard of New Forest Ladies, worthy of the years of training I'd put in then netball or hockey was my future.

Katelyn was blushing and stared down into her wine, taking a small sip, then another in some futile effort to occupy herself. She delicately set her glass down and we made eye contact again, but this time it was me who broke it.

Thankfully, the main course arrived and my 'Beef Tenderloin From Our Summer Pastures Cooked In Hay From The Grasslands' almost sent me over the edge from the mere smell alone.

When everybody finished their meals, the waiters cleared away the plates and Marco brought over more bottles of wine for the table.

"He is so gorgeous." Amanda declared, loud enough for everyone to hear and then she blushed realising she'd revealed her crush. We all laughed as she hid behind her hands.

"You should ask him to show you the local landmarks." Marie suggested, prompting murmurs of agreement from the rest.

We spent the next few minutes attempting to psyche Amanda up to approach him, but in the end she chickened out. Lucky for her, Marie possessed the biggest mouth in the entire UK ladies volleyball league and when Marco returned, she blurted out, "my friend really likes you," whilst pointing at the blonde with the big breasts. Within seconds he and Amanda were exchanging numbers.

The noise levels lessened as, hoarse throated, we became content with chatting to the girl beside us. Poor Stewart, the only man on the trip, leaned back in his seat and yawned.

The whole table heard when Katelyn's phone rang and she half turned in her seat in some futile effort at gaining privacy. "Hi babe." She said almost in a whisper but so many of the gossip hungry women at the table had suspended their conversations to eavesdrop that even I could overhear, and I was furthest away from her.

I noticed the eyes flicking over me, if I didn't already know who she was speaking to, then that alone was confirmation.

"Yeah, I arrived safe, thanks. Guess what, Allison Burbridge is coming to watch us play next week...What? No, I told you, she's the national team coach...Well, I thought I did..." she giggled and hid her face "...anything with Jennifer Aniston... Can't wait myself..."

It was excruciating and I hated being forced to listen in but like the extra glass of wine you know will do you no good, I just couldn't stop myself and lamented that everyone else had fallen silent also. The harlot was aware of it too but only went so far as placing a hopeless hand close to her mouth in a forlorn effort at preventing the sound waves from reaching my ears - Heartless bitch.

Amanda, Holly and Grace all glanced at me in quick succession and I felt the heat rising within. And I was supposed to live with this for an entire week; James ringing her, making gooey noises down the phone whilst I was in the same room with no escape? Not if I had anything to do with it! Nope, something would have to change.

I clenched my fist and stood, just as an almighty gust of wind whipped a cloud of snow against the window. "Marie, are you coming to the bathroom?"

"Say what?"

"Are you coming to the bathroom?"

"Oh, sure." She required the support of my arm to stand and almost staggered across the restaurant.

It felt relieving to get away from the table and I held the bathroom door open for my drunken friend before we approached the mirror together.

She took one look at her hair and gaped. "The fuck? Has it been like this all evening? Damn bloody wind."

"I've seen you looking more dishevelled," I smiled, "but not by much."

She shook her head and frowned. "And tonight with all these waiters...Look, I know why you needed to get away from there and I don't blame you." She gave me a comforting pat on the shoulder, "I don't think you should have to put up with *that*. Katelyn should show more discretion."

"Exactly. Thank you."

"But you won't be hurting much longer, honey, I promise. You *will* find another man and soon."

"Oh I don't think so." Another man was the last thing I wanted at the moment and, rather worryingly, I fretted it was because I was regressing again, because even now, thanks to my eavesdropping, all I could think about was James and that girl watching Jennifer Aniston movies before...

"No kidding, Jess." Marie interrupted my thoughts. "Don't think I haven't noticed how men look at you." She turned away from the mirror to look straight at me. "I mean what kind of guy doesn't like a girl with long blonde hair and a killer athlete's body. Not to mention a smile that can light up the town." She turned back. "And you're way better looking than that tart, believe me. James is clearly blind, deaf and dumb."

"Thank you, that's nice of you." I felt a little better, a tiny amount perhaps and appreciated her trying even if I didn't believe her, after all, I'd seen Katelyn and I'd also seen the reaction of most men who came anywhere near her, which made it all easier to understand, but most certainly did not make it easier.

"I just wish you'd *smile* a little more often. I hate seeing you so down like this." She paused in thought. "In fact, when was the last time you smiled?"

I hit her on the arm. "That's payback for elbowing me earlier." I sighed and changed tact. "Marie, can I bunk with you and Amanda?"

She tilted her head and gave a sympathetic smile. "Oh, how could I resist that face?"

The relief washed over me like a new lease of life. "Thank you. You have no idea how much of a lifesaver you are. This might now actually turn into a good trip."

She flapped a hand. "Looks like we'll have to push the beds together, or not. You never know...Katelyn ain't the only shameless girl on the team and if Amanda hooks up with that waiter guy, you'll have a bed to yourself."

We both laughed and now, feeling more than a little tipsy, exited the bathroom.

Thank God for Marie.

AVALANCHE

The short drive back to Mortisa took longer than expected. The snow was almost like a constant blanket from the sky, the strong wind throwing it horizontal at such high speeds it was hard to see where we were going. Stewart leaned forward at the wheel, wipers on full speed whilst driving at a walking pace. The wind slammed hard into the vehicle's flank causing the entire chassis to shake. It was terrifying, especially when trundling up the narrow, bumpy, unmade road that led to the cabins.

We exited the vehicle and found ourselves needing to lean into the wind at some obscene angle to gain traction as the snow whipped into our faces. I couldn't wait to transfer my baggage into Marie's cabin and sprawl out by the log fire with a SoupInACup until falling asleep. I was sure that as soon as I was inside and snuggled up, the wind slamming against the cabin would be comforting.

As it turned out, Amanda had decided to wait behind for an

instant date with Marco, who was finishing his shift. He promised to personally drive her back to Mortisa afterwards.

"I'll see you in a few minutes, hon." I rubbed Marie on the back and continued on the arduous path toward cabin 4 as she inclined to the right.

Katelyn, who had already run ahead to the cabin, now stood in the open threshold holding the door open for me. I ran inside and Katelyn slammed the door behind.

"No need to lock it," I said, scooping up my bag by the handle whilst taking extra care not to look at her.

"Why? You have no idea who's lurking out there." Oh, she just didn't get it, but she would pretty soon.

I decided it'd feel pretty good to look her in the eye as I spoke my next words. "I'm not staying here. So you have the place to yourself and welcome." I said it with an uncaring tone just as thunder boomed from somewhere far away. "You can lock it when I'm gone. There's no way I'm putting up with your shit for a full week."

"Excuse me?" Katelyn propped her hands on her hips in the same comical way she often did around me.

"You heard." I moved toward the door, enjoying the sound of the wheels from my bag rattling across the floorboards.

For a moment I wondered if Katelyn was about to start crying. Did she really have such desires on torturing me or was she just afraid of being alone in the dark? "Jessica, I really am trying here. Can't you see that?"

"Not interested."

She stepped in front and blocked my path. "You're not leaving!" I didn't actually hear her words. The deepest and most drawn out thunder I'd ever heard blotted out her voice; though from the movement of her lips, not to mention her lean frame stepping into my path, I could take an educated guess.

"I beg your pardon? What did you say? Did you say 'I'm not leaving'?" I pushed her out of the way, which she wasn't expecting. "Just try stopping me, bitch!"

I opened the door and a sheet of snow hit me in the face, the thunder still resounded in the air.

"Please, Jess, can't we just try and be friends again?" Now she really was crying and I was struck by how much I didn't care. I never knew I was capable of being so cold and that frightened me because I knew I was a good person. But this bitch – She brought out the very worst in me and if I stayed around her for too long then I couldn't be held responsible for what happened.

I yanked my bag over the threshold, turned to grab the door knob then spoke casually, "nope, never again," but now my own voice was barely audible, even to myself.

She didn't look at me, but rather through me or beyond me and exhibited that same look she had when I'd given her a verbal barrage after arriving; her mouth hung open, her eyes glazed over but now there was something else there too. Then the opened door shook on its hinges and whatever thunder this was sure had some power.

I turned around...

...And froze.

Trees were surging towards us on a mountain of snow cascading down from the summit.

My feet were rooted to the spot. The ground shook. Shelves clattered. The noise - Deep - Loud - Terror.

Vibrations from the floor rattled through my body.

Then the villa within my line of sight disappeared into whiteness.

The rumble turned to a roar.

The minibus was lifted by some natural or perhaps unnatural force and came hurtling towards me.

Why couldn't I move?

A blur in my periphery snapped me from my trance and then the door slammed shut and the blur threw itself upon me – Katelyn. We hit the floor with a bump. Then that same floor moved beneath us as the rage filled vibrations popped up floorboards sporadically.

For the tiniest fraction of a second there was silence as the whole world stopped.

Cacophony!

It was as though we were in the eye of a hurricane. At first the constant rumbling, deep, deep rumbling was merely to the side, where snow and trees and who knew what else crashed against the wall. And then it filled our entire world as it surged over the roof like a never ending wave. Shelves threw their contents to the floor, splintering the roar with sharper crashes. The lights flickered and then went out, plunging us into darkness, and still the crashes came, from all around but some very close and an arm was cast over me and a trembling hand grabbed my own.

And then silence.

BLACKNESS.

Everything was silent, but then in death, maybe that's expected.

Lavender - In the absence of sight and hearing, that was the one sensation that pervaded my senses more than anything else.

And the darkness and quiet of the afterlife embellished that sweet and fruity heavenly scent many times over.

Only, it wasn't the afterlife because the warm air from Katelyn's nose pricked at the fine hairs on my neck and that air felt warm and as my eyes adjusted to the dark I saw two green eyes looking back at me. No, it wasn't heaven.

For how long had we been on the floor, huddling together? There was no way of knowing; seconds, minutes, hours?

Katelyn's arm jerked, or was it mine, or both? Well at least I wasn't dead but then maybe that might have been preferential to this alternative.

"Jessica? Are you ok?" The whisper came from so close.

"A slight headache...um, feel a bit sick."

"Me too...disorientated."

Something moved below my neck and then I saw it was Katelyn freeing her arm.

Where was *my* arm? I couldn't feel it. Panic set in. Then Katelyn sat up and I could trace the entire length from shoulder to hand and reasoned Katelyn had been lying on top of it, cutting the circulation. I flexed my fingers, elbow and circled my arm about the shoulder joint. The feeling, I hoped, would soon come back when the circulation returned, though how long that would be I couldn't tell. "How heavy are you?"

She straightened and spoke with an accusatory tone. "How heavy am I? How heavy are you? I can barely feel my arm here."

I could make out her outline in the dark. "You can't feel *your* arm? You've crushed mine. Lose some bloody weight!"

"Why don't *you* lose some bloody weight!"

I sat up and blinked, not that it made a difference. "Can you see anything?" The larger shapes in the distance were slightly recognisable; the kitchen countertop, pillar, TV perhaps.

"Um, not really. I can see you but that's about it."

I felt a hand touch my arm and then Katelyn began rubbing it through the thick layers of winter clothing. If I could feel this then the circulation was returning. She slid closer and massaged my arm with both hands, the smell of lavender returning, not completely unwelcome considering. In fact the small human contact felt comforting after what had just happened, even if it was Katelyn.

What *had* just happened?

"Katelyn, what the heck was that?"

"Not too sure, an avalanche would be the logical guess?"

"I think, um, maybe you're right. I remember seeing the minibus flying at me."

The feeling in my arm returned, the disorientation was ceasing and I remembered I despised this girl whom fate insisted on keeping me near. She had stopped massaging me and now just clung to my arm as if doing so would keep us safe. I snatched my arm away and shuffled across the floor into some space.

"Oh, you're so welcome, Jess!" Her outline climbed to its feet.

"Welcome? Welcome for what?"

"Hmm, let me think for a minute...For saving your life perhaps?" Her hand was extended out in front like she was reaching for something, a wall or pillar to hold on to. "Where are you?"

"For saving my life?" Was she serious? Sure she'd closed the door, but I was about to do that anyway. Sure she'd pulled me away from the shelves that crashed from the wall, but even if they'd hit me, they wouldn't have killed me. The worst that would've happened is that maybe my volleyball playing days would be over, which under the circumstances would not have made much difference. "Being alone with you is a fate worse than death."

"If I hadn't stopped you leaving then you'd be outside freezing to death in the snow right about now." She sounded more distant than earlier and I guessed she was now in the kitchen. But although she had a point, I'd never say so.

"When you stopped me, there was no way you could have known it was an avalanche, so stop taking credit for things you couldn't help. You're an accidental hero, which hardly counts."

"Says who?"

"I don't know...Me for one."

"Well then maybe it's just fate we're both here together."

"Oh shut up! I don't believe in fate. And you're still a bitch."

A distant thump signalled that Katelyn had walked into something. "Ouch!"

I couldn't help but laugh.

"Now you can just shut up. At least I'm trying to find a light switch."

How stupid was she? "The lights were on before the avalanche right?"

"Yeah, so?"

"Well then obviously the lights are *still* switched on." After a protracted silence, clearly she still hadn't got it. "The fuse has been struck. How stupid are you?"

"Oh. Well, what does that mean we have to do?"

"You still live with your parents don't you?" I asked, knowing the answer.

"Oh, I'm so sorry, Jess, for never having lived through an avalanche before. And no, I do not live with my bloody parents."

"We need to find the fuse box and flick the switch. And I've never lived through a bloody avalanche either, but certain things are just obvious."

I pulled out my phone, thinking the bright screen would suffice as a makeshift torch. I waved it around and saw the distant shape of Katelyn, hands on hips. If she was not pleased then that made two of us. "There's just one floor in this place, no cellar, so I'm guessing the fuse box is somewhere in the kitchen, maybe inside a cupboard."

An extra light flicked on, Katelyn having brought her own phone to life and we opened each cupboard in turn, shining the lights inside in search of the fuse box. Katelyn stooped down and reached inside a cupboard. After a second...

...Light.

The abrupt brightness was a shock to my eyes, causing me to squint and my first sight was of Katelyn on all fours, her head still inside a cupboard. Even in her winter jacket, I had to admit, she possessed the kind of curves men lusted over.

She moved out from the cupboard and scrambled to her feet. "What?" She asked after a few seconds.

I must have had a glassy eyed expression but I shook it away. "Nothing. Um, I was just thinking about how shitty this situation is."

"It is." She agreed with a nod.

I wandered around the cabin, surveying the damage. The avalanche had knocked two out of three shelves clean off their brackets; the third had its contents thrown to the floor, which was now a total mess. An old style clock was smashed to bits along with several ornaments and framed photographs of the town and region. Big thick volumes on Italy, which could have caused damage had they hit me, now sat haphazard across the floor, which proved the sheer force behind the natural disaster we'd sustained, yet also the workmanship of the structure we were in, for mercifully, it was still standing. The place was a mess but far from beyond restoration because from what I could see at least, the structure was still sound.

There were two large windows on either side of the cabin, all unnaturally high in the wall, which would serve to allow direct sunlight into the room. From the wall the avalanche struck, the view was now nothing but a dull snow colour pressed hard against the glass as if it was so packed in against the side no light could seep through. Darkness was the result. The fact the windows were so high probably meant the wall had taken the sting from the avalanche and had saved them from shattering. Either that or the glass was too thick for the snow to penetrate, either way, I was not qualified to judge. One thing was certain and that was the snow was piled high. But how high?

"I know what you're thinking, Jess. The snow went over us. We're entombed in here." Katelyn spoke from as far away as our tomb allowed, leaning against the kitchen work surface in the far corner, not a hint of fear or apprehension in her tone or on her face, from what I could see at least.

I took one step forward. "You really think?"

"Yes."

"And you're not worried?"

"No." She stepped out from the kitchen and looked up to the windows. "Well not really. They'll be sure to find us and we'll have a cool story to tell when we get home."

I hoped she was right about that. At the very least, I was stuck here with Katelyn for the night.

Then I remembered – Marie – I was meant to be heading to her cabin. My arms tensed up as I looked around and behind, searching in haste for something, or some way out but I wasn't sure what or where.

"Jess, what's the matter?"

"Marie. N...No, everybody. Are they ok? Marie was expecting me. I have to speak to her." I was holding onto the pillar by this point, wanting nothing more than to flee, to breathe fresh air, to know they were ok.

Katelyn marched towards me and grabbed ahold of my shoulders. "Jess, calm down. I'm sure they're all fine. *We're* ok, aren't we? The cabin held out. I'm sure they all did."

"Yes, it did." Logic, relief, breathe. "Yes, yes it did, yes."

Her hands were still on me, gently kneading and rubbing my shoulders, which was unbelievably soothing after almost losing my mind in a fit of hysteria. "Better now?" She whispered in a way that was just as calming.

I nodded, almost smiled and stepped away.

She hesitated, sighed, then pulled out her phone. "Look, why don't you phone Marie and I'll phone Dorothy...Check everyone's alive."

It was a good idea and so I looked up 'Big Mouth' and called. No sound. It was dead. I checked the screen and found the reason. "I can't get any signal."

"Me neither." Katelyn groaned, slipping the phone back in her pocket.

I kicked a piece of broken glass across the floor. "Oh just bloody perfect!"

"Look, this is Italy. I'm sure they're used to this kind of thing happening, especially in a ski resort. Everybody will be fine and they'll be around here soon enough with a tractor or plough or something."

"You'd better be right."

After unknown minutes pottering uselessly around the disordered cabin, I realised I'd eventually come to stand in the far corner of the room, where the couch faced the TV and that Katelyn was back loitering in the kitchen from where she now perched against the countertop staring into nothing. It was like we both automatically gravitated to the place as far away from the other as possible. There was something about her that just made me uncomfortable. Even though I was pretty much over James, or at least that's what I kept telling myself, I still felt there was some other reason she made me feel uneasy. Somehow, I doubted I'd ever feel relaxed around her.

I stumped toward the door and Katelyn perked up as I did.

"What are you doing?" She demanded, now hurrying over.

"I'm just curious. Maybe it's not as deep out as we think. Besides, my bag's outside. It's right by the door." My hand hovered over the doorknob and Katelyn pulled it away, in fact it was almost a yank, which took me by surprise and my mouth hung half open. "Excuse me, bitch?"

"Take a look up there." She jabbed a finger up high toward the windows. "We're covered, ok. If you open that door then how do you know we won't be engulfed?" She took the key from her pocket and locked the door. "And will you stop calling me bitch!"

Well, that was the first time I'd ever seen Katelyn angry, or perhaps mildly irritated would be a better description. It was bound to happen at some point the way I'd been speaking to her, deserved as it was. Though she may have had a point, again, even if I hated to admit it. There was no knowing what might happen if I opened that door and I hated the thought of being overwhelmed by freezing cold snow. The only problem was my nightclothes were in that bag, not to mention everything else which I needed.

"I have some spare nightclothes in mine."

My mouth half gaped again. "How, how did you..."

"...Because it's late and it's obvious." She shook her head playfully and tutted. "They'll be a tiny bit too large but you can borrow them."

I cleared my throat. "That's...that's very kind of you. Thank you." And that wasn't easy for me to say, in fact it was even harder for me to be looking at her as I said it and I don't even think she expected it.

"Um, yes." She almost stammered after recovering from the shock and then she turned and headed for the hearth, where her bag still sat, before unzipping it and proceeding to rummage through. "Mind, um, not that I think sleeping will be easy, considering I'm trapped in an avalanche with a girl who wants to kill me, but I can think of no better way to pass the time."

I tried to think up something not completely mundane to fill the silence and managed to come up with something suitably boring. "If you're right then hopefully by the time we wake they'll have a plough out here and we can go skiing."

"Correct. And you can move in with Marie." She passed me some bright green stretchy pants and a cute little red t-shirt that had the word, 'Perfect' stamped on it.

"Thanks." I held the top across my chest to measure it against myself, inhaling the sweet lavender that unfurled with it. She sure was curvy, all right, and I knew the t-shirt would put me to shame. I felt my face soften. "I don't actually want to *kill* you, Katelyn. I'd happily settle for seeing your shoulder permanently separated."

She cracked up. Well, at least *she* could laugh at the damned sorry situation. Then, after a few seconds, I began laughing myself, which amazed me.

"Are you cold?" She asked after almost a minute.

"No. I'm guessing the snow is acting as some kind of an insulator." I thought about igloos. I didn't know the science behind them but snow obviously acted in some way to keep the heat trapped within. Or perhaps, keeping in mind the location up here in the mountains, the cabins were just exceptionally well made. They had survived being pounded by an avalanche, or at least *our* cabin had. Not knowing how the others fared was horrible. "But I'm not taking any chances. I'll put your nightclothes on underneath and sleep in my jacket too."

"Yes, maybe that's a good idea." Katelyn brought out a toiletry bag.

"I don't mean to be cheeky but..."

"...but you'd like to know if I have a spare toothbrush?"

How did she do that? Maybe it was just plain obvious. "Yes. Do you?"

She fumbled around inside the bag and passed me a toothbrush still in its packaging.

"Thanks."

She held my eye contact. "I'm not all bad, you know."

"Hey, I haven't forgotten anything."

I went to the bathroom, which was the only place in the entire cabin that offered any kind of privacy, and studied my reflection in the mirror. "Man, I look haggard." And I didn't like it one bit. The day had taken its toll on my features and I felt as tired as I looked. Though, I surmised as I squeezed paste onto Katelyn's brush and began working over my teeth, it was quite reasonable considering the day I'd had; the long plane journey, drive through the mountains, an avalanche and last but not least, being forced by human as well as supernatural contrivances to shack up with my worst enemy. Katelyn, despite everything, didn't however look as haggard as me. How did she do it? Genetics? Maybe she was just one of the lucky ones. And that my hair should appear dull and ragged when hers was still so straight and thick and shiny. And it wasn't just my hair, but my skin also looked dull, which I really hated, whilst hers was smooth and clear, which I also hated. Still, it was good of her to give me a toothbrush because she sure didn't have to. I'd be sure to buy her a new one, given I really didn't want to be beholden to her, not even for something as small as that. But who was *she* to prevent me from retrieving my bag from outside? Hmm, maybe she did have a point about that, maybe. And pretty soon she'd be playing in the national team. How long had it been since we left the Rosa Alpina? I checked the time on my phone. Almost three hours. Bloody hell.

I spat the foam into the sink and turned on the tap. The water had a slight brown tint to it, but that shouldn't be much of a problem. I'd seen that happen from time to time living out in the country and before long it always changed back to normal.

I laid the toothbrush out on the sink, ruffled my hair in an attempt to conceal it's dishevelled look, conceded to straighten it, scrutinised my appearance with a tilted head and a frown before returning to the messed up look, but not so messed it looked deliberate, all the while regretting the absence of my bag along with my oils, hair tie and everything else. Finally I sighed, opened the door and stepped into the cabin's main room...

...To where Katelyn was in the process of peeling off her hoody.

I froze as the garment snapped over her head to reveal Katelyn in only a black lace bra and panties.

She stood facing the hearth, so that her side profile was visible to my eyes. Her long slender legs stopped at an ass that could have been carved from alabaster. Her belly was perfectly flat with the slightest hint of obliques. My eyes though were drawn to her breasts, large and round, impossibly high in her bra, its material stretched out impressively and I had to swallow because my mouth was suddenly dry. She fanned out her mane, a movement that momentarily distracted my eyes from where they'd been, before she proceeded to tie her long, loosed brown hair into a tail. For reasons I didn't know my eyes glanced back down, but not for long.

It all happened so fast, in less time than it had taken for the bathroom door to close, and as it fell into its frame with a click she turned calmly around to find me standing in an open space.

"Oh, hey, you all right?"

For reasons I couldn't fathom my right knee was trembling. "Excuse me?"

She stepped forward a pace but I was already looking at the floor and now turned toward the bed where my borrowed nightclothes were neatly set out, although the stretchy pants were at a slight angle, but hey, wasn't that an interesting font scrawled on the t-shirt; red and green combo, very colourful.

"You kind of looked confused, or in a trance, or something. Is there something in the bathroom I should be aware of?" She was now fully facing me, at least I sensed she was, but I didn't look up and if I answered her rhetorical question I was unaware of it. "You all done in there?"

"Um, yes, I'm all done in there." I adjusted the valance, tugging it down an inch and, ridiculously, patted the cuff on the end of Katelyn's borrowed stretchy pants before making them perfectly straight on the bed.

Finally, I felt the breeze hit my back as she headed for the bathroom, her bare feet making light pattering sounds on the floorboards, the outline of something red she'd since slipped on a blur in my periphery. The door closed and I stripped off my clothes, flung them to the chair and threw on the borrowed nightclothes, inhaling lavender as I did. As anticipated, I was somewhat less of a woman than she in certain areas and I retrieved my jacket from the chair and zipped it up over the t-shirt, jumping under the covers before she returned.

I lay, listened to the rhythm of my breathing, the muffled sound of brushing in the near distance and clenched my fists around the hem of the duvet.

Please God, but please tell me she didn't catch me gawping at her, please, please, please.

Was I though? Is that what I was doing? Truth is, I didn't exactly know. But what if I had been and what if she saw me? I winced and felt my toes curling - Well, she shouldn't have been standing around almost naked then. Clearly that woman didn't have the same issues as I had about being undressed around other girls.

And so she had a hot body, I was honest enough to admit that - Long, lean, athletic, powerful, tanned. It helped to understand what I was against here, just why I'd lost James and my place on the team. She had some kind of genetic advantage which I, being a mere mortal could never hope to compete with.

I lay in bed, my mouth was dry and there was a fluttery feeling in my belly. Then, as I pictured Katelyn standing by the hearth, tying her hair back, breasts gently rising and falling in rhythm with her breathing, my hand slowly searched down toward my pussy and I glanced a finger along my outer walls and onto my clit. My body bucked from the contact and I couldn't understand anything – I was soaking wet. And so I pressed harder and then...

...Katelyn flung open the door, startling me and my hands were back clutching the hems, and I pulled the cover over my face.

She turned out the lights, climbed into her bed and we lay there.

WHITE

$\mathcal{T}$he only sleep I managed was sporadic. The first time I woke I put down to being mere feet away from Katelyn, who breathed quite heavy during the night with intermittent snores that sprung me from my slumber. I had no idea girls snored, even though it wasn't proper snoring. I think on a few occasions she woke herself and then we both lay there, staring silently into the dark - Or perhaps it was all just my imagination, I was tired, after all.

Later, I woke after a dream of skiing down a steep slope. I lost control and ended up falling from a cliff into an abyss.

Then, several times, I awoke due to the sheer drop in temperature. It must have happened during the night for reasons I was not qualified to guess. Out of habit I always envelop my feet at the end of the duvet because I find it provides warmth and a feeling of comfort. Still, my toes were bordering on being frozen and my fingertips experienced a similar discomfort. Worst of all, my left ear, which had remained exposed to the room, iced up and all too frequently during the uncomfortable night I found myself shivering.

I yawned and checked the time on my phone - Just gone 5 am.

"Katelyn?" I whispered, expecting no answer to be forthcoming.

"Yeah?" Returned the hiss.

"Are you awake?" I asked, feeling stupid as soon as I'd spoken.

"Of course, silly." In fact she sounded alert.

"Can you sleep?"

"No, not really. It's so fucking cold."

"I know. I keep waking up."

"Me too."

"I'm thinking of getting up."

"Why are you still whispering?" She said louder with a hint of jest in the tone.

I laughed. "I don't know."

I threw off the covers and fumbled through my clothes which were slumped over the chair and tried to find the items that made the most logical sense to dress in first, like my bra and underwear. It was hard in the pitch black, but damn it, I would do it.

"Here, let me put the light on for you." I heard Katelyn step out from her bed and begin treading across the floor.

"No! Katelyn, it's all right. I'll manage." I'd taken off my jacket and Katelyn's t-shirt whilst rummaging around for my bra and I now sat naked on the bed, all except for her stretchy pants and even though I faced away from her, I still didn't want the light turning on.

"Don't be silly. You need to see to get dressed."

I was about to interject but then the room filled with light and my head with self-consciousness. "Um, thanks."

"That should be easier for you now." She walked back to her bed and as I leaned forward clutching myself, I heard a bag unzip and then what I assumed to be Katelyn sifting through her own clothes. "Can't have you sitting there all naked, Jess, not in this cold."

She didn't make much noise behind me, which was regrettable, on this occasion at least, because I could have used the distraction. A radio, the boiling of a kettle or anything else would have been convenient, but there was nothing, just the two of us pottering about in silence. She'd obviously already seen I was naked – How could she not have? Indeed, she'd as good as said so and I didn't know how to feel about that other than perhaps a little awkward.

No wonder I couldn't find my bra; I'd knocked it to the floor whilst I was rummaging through everything. I leaned forward with one arm covering my breasts and plucked it up with my free hand before attempting to attach the thing in my usual complex yet practiced way, just like I always did in the changing rooms. It made no difference that I faced away from her and she couldn't see my boobs anyway, or that my face was flushing red, even in this suppressive temperature. Why was she being so silent? Was she looking at me? I attached my bra and shivered as my frozen fingers made contact with the flesh on my back.

I didn't want another night like that again, if it could even be called a night, for no sleep was had.

"Bagsy the bathroom first." Katelyn declared as she bounded around the bed with a heap of clothes and a towel slung over her arm.

The bathroom door closed behind her and I stood and

dressed minus the obstacle that was Katelyn. Within a minute I could hear the muffled sound of water patting down from the shower and I wished I'd thought of that first. At least we'd been provided with fresh towels so I wouldn't need to borrow one off Katelyn.

There was a sudden shrill cry from the bathroom but I didn't bother to investigate. The last thing I needed was to check in on her in the shower, not that I thought *she* had any insecurities about such things - Why would she with a body like that?

After a few minutes she emerged stomping into the cabin, grumpy expression in tow and two towels wrapped around her. "Don't use that bloody shower. The thing went suddenly freezing and the water's the colour of mud."

I felt the side of my mouth involuntarily curl upwards as a slight warmth, from the thought of her discomfort, flooded through my body. Despite the water temperature suddenly free falling, and turning to mud, it hadn't stopped her suffering through it regardless. Vanity, I thought, and the first sign of humanity I'd come to witness in this individual. Maybe she was human after all, maybe.

She dumped herself on her bed and sulked as water from her head dripped over the towel wrapped around her body. She then produced a third towel and proceeded to pat her hair with it. "I feel dirtier now than when I got in and even colder, if that's possible."

"I'll keep that in mind." I couldn't help but giggle at her misfortune but made sure she didn't see it.

I checked my phone for any sign of messages or attempts to contact us. No messages, missed calls or bars of signal. So much for going skiing today, this whole sorry situation was getting steadily worse. "Hey, there's no sign of any rescue." I said in a tone full of gloom whilst staring up at the windows and their wall of snow pressing against them. I'd envisioned the heavy hums of diggers lifting away giant mounds of snow with their scoops, breaking us free. Marie, Dorothy and everybody else were all there waiting to hear our stories. Not so much, as it turned out, at least not yet.

"Huh? Oh, give them time." She said with no hint of worry, which gave me confidence. She was getting changed now and I decided I didn't want her to catch me gawking again. In fact, I didn't want to catch myself staring at her, if that is what I was doing, for I couldn't be sure. One embarrassment was enough for this trip, so I occupied myself by turning on the TV and flicking through the channels. Most of them were grainy but watchable.

I stopped on a local news bulletin where a female reporter was standing, microphone in hand, in a pretty snow covered town. She wore warm clothes against the weather as the snow fell heavy, covering the roads and pretty much everything else. The image flickered and fuzzed and she spoke in lightning quick Italian, which made garnering any information difficult. However, there could be no misinterpreting the complete lack of activity, or any movement whatsoever in the scene to her rear. Wherever that place was would have to call in a few snow days. Then the camera panned to the right and I was immediately struck by something recognisable; it was Strada Micura de Ru and the Rosa Alpina was there with snow heaped against the entrance. And then other Cortina landmarks like the town square and large church which dominated the centre came into focus.

"Hey, Katelyn, I think they're running a report from the town."

"What? Really?" She bounded over whilst zipping up her jacket.

The reporter was gesturing around her head with an arm as if signalling something that happened over there and over there. Then the camera focused sidewards to a knoll of snow piled next to a building and the nine or ten locals gathered around, scratching their heads with uncertain expressions. Then it cut to a pre-shot image of an espresso bar, its front window conspicuous by the Fiat 500 that was now inserted through it.

My heart sank. "Looks like the damn avalanche made it all the way to the town centre." How bad had it been? Had anybody been hurt, or worse?

The owner of the espresso bar was pitching snow out through the gaping hole in his building, which would take a while with his one shovel. Then the picture cut to a small convoy of ploughs battling along a snowy road at a snail's pace.

"At least they're coming. How many is there; three, four?" Katelyn asked as the report ended.

"Looked like four of them." And that was a good sign, even if a few holiday cabins would hardly be the priority over the entire town which had also suffered, I knew the stupid snow would soon be cleared away and then we could check on everybody else. I just hoped that time would arrive soon.

For the first time I noticed the steam from my mouth as I breathed. The cabin was freezing and although I now walked around in an attempt to generate warmth, whilst wearing the same thick layers of clothing I'd worn yesterday, something needed to be done about the temperature.

Two large radiators were attached to the walls; one beside the bathroom entrance and the other behind the couch. "Any idea how to turn these things on?" I called over to Katelyn who was busy searching the kitchen cupboards.

"No switch on them?"

"No."

"There'll be a thermostat somewhere." She said pulling items from the cupboards and placing them on the countertop.

The thermostat was in a store cupboard which also contained the usual stuff you'd expect to find in a rented cabin; ironing board, vacuum cleaner and a bunch of aerosols for cleaning and polishing. I always thought thermostats worked by judging the temperature of the room and acting accordingly to keep it within pre-specified ranges. Either that or you could turn them off and on as required. I guessed that if the cabins had remained unoccupied for any period of time then the warden would have turned the heating off to save power, though ensured it was returned in time for our arrival. If that was the case then the warden had failed here, or otherwise the avalanche had tripped the switch. Anyway, I flicked the switch upwards from a 'o' symbol to one that resembled a radiator. I also increased the temperature to as high as it would go and conceded I probably should have done that last night.

The kitchen countertop now had a weird array of stuff pulled out from the cupboards. Saucepans, frying pans, cutlery, plates, dishes, cups and odd looking utensils I'd never seen before in my life – Probably weird Italian cooking gadgets. Katelyn stood amongst it all, hands on hips and a giant frown. "You see this? This is all the food we have. Fucking self-catering..."

I'd seen the amount of food Katelyn liked to pile on her plate. Come to think of it, the entire volleyball team could have eaten for England, myself included. I approached the counter where she'd gathered what little 'food' there was into a small space in the centre. We had salt, vinegar, mustard, a few tea bags and coffee beans. I held the latter up and examined the pack.

"Well at least we have a grinder." I remarked, gesturing to the device somewhere amongst the rest.

She held up some other, tiny kettle looking device. "Yep, and this here's a mocha pot, which I hear are popular in these parts."

"Cool, you know how to work it?"

"Nope. But more to the point, Jess, we don't have any food."

"And you've checked everywhere?"

"Yes."

I pointed to her oversized traveller's bag by her bed. "Please tell me you have a banquet in there. Any snacks or...anything?"

"We were supposed to be going shopping for groceries today before skiing, the whole group was." Her face lit up like she'd remembered something. "I do have a few bars of chocolate; Galaxy Milk. I've always been addicted to that...Couldn't survive long here without it."

I sighed and conceded, "it's something at least." Then I remembered and gestured to the door. "In my bag...I have some hot chocolate and a couple packs of SoupInACup."

Katelyn laughed.

"What?"

"SoupInACup? Looks like we both have our guilty pleasures."

"Hey, how dare you disrespect SoupInACup. You've obviously never tried it...Call yourself a student?"

"I'm sure it's tasty. I'm just worried about the lack of nutrition. We don't have much between us and I'm only eating mustard as a last resort." She glanced at the label. "Ugh, and it's *English* mustard too, in Italy of all places, that's like the strongest mustard there is."

Katelyn began tidying the countertop, replacing the items

she'd brought out. Meanwhile I realised I hadn't yet drunk my customary two glasses of morning water so I held a glass under the tap and turned it on. After a short pause, followed by a high pitched rattle that emanated from the pipes, a heavy brown tinted sludge began filling the glass.

"Um, I'm not too sure this water's safe to drink." I held the sludge up, not quite believing what I was seeing.

Katelyn bobbed her head up from below the countertop. "Yuck! That's worse than the shower. There's no way I'm drinking that."

This was getting bad now. We could be trapped inside the cabin all day. What were we supposed to drink?

I plonked myself on the couch and exhaled. It wasn't merely the lack of food and water but there was nothing to occupy our time with either. The mind needed stimulation and my books and music were in my bag. And it wasn't only that, but it was still bloody freezing in here.

I checked the temperature of the radiator behind me and grimaced. "Oh, to have a break around here. The heating isn't working."

"You switched it on didn't you?"

"Yes!"

"Any sign of a boiler anywhere?" Katelyn asked.

"Nope, not that I've seen."

"Then I'm guessing there must be one big communal boiler that heats water for the entire place."

"I have no idea." I shrugged. "It'll be outside in the Warden's closet or something." If such a place or man existed. "Not that I'm an expert..." I trailed off.

So now we had no food, no water and no heat. Add sleep to the list and this whole trip wasn't going too great. Not to mention I was stuck in an ever increasingly claustrophobic shack with Katelyn – Marvellous.

I jumped up suddenly from the couch. "I want my bag, Katelyn. Would you unlock the door." I demanded in a tone with more of an edge than intended.

"And just when I thought we were getting along so well." She said, taking a few cautious steps in my direction.

But I wasn't having any of that, not now. "Look, I want my things. You have no right to keep them from me. If the snow cascades in on us then quite honestly, I couldn't give a shit. It'll just get a tiny bit colder in here, that's all. I'm sure we'll really notice the difference." I was scrutinising her for any reaction as the words came out, the only visible response being her hands that gravitated towards those curvaceous hips - Hourglass or what, they were almost ridiculous, as was she. "We have no drinkable water. So the only option is to drink the bloody snow that's piled up out there anyway, we'll have to open the door or die of thirst, so there."

After a few seconds, in which she seemed to be giving it thought, she finally conceded. "You have a point there, Jess."

"Of course. So open the bloody door." I tried to appear at least semi-threatening. Though the truth was that if it came to a struggle between the two of us, there'd only be one winner and I doubted it'd be me.

"There's no need to be so hostile. I'm just trying to get by you know. Preferably without being engulfed in snow." She stepped toward the door and removed the key from her pocket. "Are you ready for this?"

"Ready when you are." I stood a little way to the side and assumed she'd succeeded in making me more paranoid about the level of danger than what actually existed.

She turned the key and I heard the distinct click of the lock mechanism before she slowly turned the handle and inched the door inward. A few inches was all it took and Katelyn leapt back as the weight of snow pressing against the door flung it wide open.

"My God." She yelped as snow tipped inside. It fell in from the top two feet of the opening where it was less compressed than below. A small but growing pile of the stuff began collecting inside, hardly life threatening, and my suitcase sat wedged in a cavity at the bottom. "Well, we got your bag." She said, displaying perfectly straight teeth that must've been recently whitened - Vanity, you see.

"I'll dig it out." I fetched a saucepan from the kitchen and began scooping around the edges until the handle became free. It was jammed in tight where the more compressed snow at the base had smashed the suitcase against the door. The door itself had a chunk of wood taken out where I guessed the hard plastic from the case had collided with it.

"Here, let me help you." Katelyn said, wrapping her fingers around the handle next to my own. Her cold hands made me shiver and gone was the smell of lavender, now replaced by a definite smell of earth she had the shower to thank for.

We didn't want to heave the thing and trigger our own mini avalanche inside the cabin and so it required several light tugs and careful twists to gently lever it out. And then it came free to reveal a suitcase sized hole in the compressed snow.

I looked at Katelyn and, not for the first time since being stuck with her, felt a small amount of gratitude. I smiled, I'm not sure why, but it certainly didn't hurt my face. "Thank you, Katelyn."

"You're welcome." She smiled back before I turned around and wheeled the bag toward the couch.

We filled as many containers as possible with snow from the floor inside the cabin until, finally, we were able to shove the door closed. We used a total of five large saucepans, a washing up bowl, two mixing bowls and several drinking glasses, compressing as much snow as we could into the containers as I knew we'd have less volume once it melted. Plenty more where that came from.

"Now what?" Katelyn asked, staring at the harmless fluffy looking stuff that had caused us so much trouble.

"Well I guess we can either wait for it to melt, which in this room would take forever. Or we could give it a little help." I gestured to the gas stove.

"Gas it is." Katelyn beamed, taking hold of one of the saucepans and placing it over the hob. She turned the knob and pressed the ignite button. The spark flashed and was accompanied by the familiar clicking sound but after several seconds it hadn't ignited. "What's wrong with this thing?"

"Is the gas coming out?" I moved my head closer to the stove and listened for the hiss of gas. "I can't hear anything."

"Oh that's just great." She took hold of the pan handle and banged it against the stove's metal grid, accomplishing nothing.

I exhaled and pinched at the flesh between my eyes. "Now we can add *no gas* to the ever expanding list of basic things we don't have." This was turning into a real joke, bordering on becoming a nightmare, and it was still early in the day. There was still adequate time for other calamities to take place. I opened the top drawer, brandished the rolling pin, "it's time to go caveman," and began crushing the snow beneath one end of the heavy wooden kitchen utensil. Gradually, after several minutes the snow turned to a drinkable slush which made up a little over half its original volume. Snow, when melted, did not go far.

Katelyn brought over two glasses and I poured in the slush.

"To escaping this rotten cabin." I'd been about to make a toast *to Italy*, but then changed my mind at the last moment and the word 'escaping' came out 'itscaping.' Oh well.

Her mouth curled downwards as she clinked her glass and then we both stared at the gunk. I for one had the feeling of jumping off the high board for the first time, but it was only water.

"I'm thinking this won't do our core temperatures much good." Katelyn said apathetically.

"You're right. But what's the alternative? We could drink the mud or die of thirst if that's any better?"

She pursed her lips together. "It looks like our only options are dying of thirst, dying from earth poisoning or dying from the cold."

"Look, I accept that *none* of this is ideal, but I take your point." My mouth was dry and I realised it was last night when I'd last had a drink and that drink had been alcohol and lots of it. I would by now be dehydrated. "If you want to die of dehydration, Katelyn, then please go right ahead. See if I give a shit." That last comment had more than just a touch of urgency to it and I tipped the glass to my lips and shivered as the freezing slush ran down my throat. "Oh, that went straight to my brain." Still, it was vaguely passable.

She'd set her full glass down on the countertop and watched with a scowl as I drank. "Look, Jess, at the very least, it looks like we're stuck in here all day, so can we please try and be civil to each other?" Her hands gravitated toward her hips again. She was so predictable. It had gone from being funny at first but was starting to irritate me now. "Don't think I don't see it in your face. Every time you speak to me, it's through gritted teeth. I know we have a history but there's no need for us to be at each other's throats."

I slammed the glass down. "And there's no need to steal my boyfriend, bitch!" It was an automatic response and I watched as her head jutted back in shock and I wondered if having no retort pained her. She stole my boyfriend – What was there she could say in defence? But there was no way, no way in hell I was about to let *her* take the high ground with me. Not after what she'd done and the pain she'd put me through.

The problem was that there was nowhere I could go to get away from her, not even for a few minutes, save for the bathroom, which would have to do for the time being, so I headed over with some freshly melted water to brush my teeth and spend a few precious moments away from her company.

When I returned to the main room, an obvious tension remained between us, which suited me. Katelyn had assumed her usual distant position, leaning against the kitchen countertop as she looked sadly down at the floor. Her glass of water was now empty. At least she'd taken a drink and I found myself surprised I actually cared.

I occupied myself for at least an hour, pacing from one side of the cabin to the next; again and again and again. Neither of us spoke. We didn't even look at each other.

The steam from my mouth was thicker than I'd noticed before; an indicator that the cabin's temperature was falling further. It certainly felt colder despite the amount of plodding around I was doing.

Throughout this time Katelyn had barely moved and only made the occasional yawning or coughing sound.

Finally, I stopped still and glanced over at her. "Katelyn?"

She tilted her head up and smiled. "Jess?"

"Aren't you cold?"

"I've never been so cold in all my life." It was the way she said it that gave me concern, for the words could easily be misinterpreted as exaggerating, but there was none of that in her tone, only certainty.

I don't know why I did it. I don't know why I cared. Maybe it was the natural feminine instinct within me. An instinct that deemed I must care for another human being in difficulty. But I walked into the kitchen and approached her. She watched me all the way with a look that suggested she was unsure of what I was about to do and the truth is that I wasn't even sure myself. When I arrived in front of her I opened out my arms and pulled her toward me into an embrace. I didn't hesitate and neither did she, her powerful frame shivered in my arms. Her limbs felt stiff, like treacle left in the refrigerator. My cheek pressed against hers and the cold from her face transferred a shiver to me.

"You're so cold." I rubbed her back through thick layers of clothing and her head came to rest upon my shoulder. I recalled how, the night before, she'd rubbed my arm to restore circulation and now I rubbed her arms in a forlorn hope at generating warmth.

"Thank you." She whispered, pulling away after several minutes. Her cheeks were a touch lighter than usual, but what caught my attention was the single tear that rolled down her face. She turned away, suddenly embarrassed, and her hand moved upwards but there was no hiding it from me.

I didn't think for one minute I'd actually warmed her up, not even in the slightest, but sometimes a little human contact can do so much more.

My eyes glanced over to the fireplace and to the small pile of logs stacked beside it. "I think it's about time we threw some of that wood in the fire and try lighting the thing."

A box of firelighters and some matches lay on a shelf next to the logs. I put a couple of the small blocks on the fire grate and they ignited easily. Katelyn came over with a bundle of logs in her arms and placed them over the flame. It didn't take long for the logs to catch fire and the heat generated as it took form was a blessing.

We brought the couch over, each taking an end and plonking it as close to the fire as practical.

"We'll need to ration those logs, just in case, you know, we're here longer." I stared at the pile that seemed to have taken a severe hit by the lifting of a mere four logs. "Do we not have any coal or anything else?" I knew that coal burned at a much higher temperature than wood and lasted considerably longer.

"I've not seen any coal, just what we have here." Katelyn confirmed as she went to the kitchen and brought back a saucepan of snow. "It'll have to do."

"Let's pray we're not prisoners here for much longer then, and nice thinking about heating the water." I gestured to the pan and smiled to myself. "I think this calls for some hot chocolate."

"I would never say no to that." Katelyn leaned forward on her perch and held the pan over the flame.

I rummaged through my suitcase and brought over two sachets of hot chocolate. Five minutes later the snow had changed to steaming water and we filled two large mugs and tipped in the sachet contents. The powder dissolved into the water to create beautiful yet improvised hot chocolate.

"My first ever cup of hot snow chocolate." Katelyn said.

"Don't you mean snow hot chocolate?" I corrected her.

She took a sip and narrowed her eyes. "No, I think hot snow chocolate has a better ring to it."

"Oh, you really think, do you?" I gave her a nudge with my knee.

We sat, mostly in silence, but a comfortable one and enjoyed the warmth, then Katelyn spoke. "I think this is my favourite part of the trip so far."

It was strange, but I had to agree with her, even if I couldn't say it. "This whole trip isn't exactly what I'd call *team bonding*."

Katelyn thought for a bit. "Maybe it is."

"What do you mean by that?"

"Nothing."

I AWOKE WITH A START, MY HEAD NESTLED AGAINST THE ARM rest of the couch that lay in front of the fire's dying embers. It was warm, thank God, and my sleep had been trouble free.

To my side, Katelyn was stretching out her arms, her head snuggled upon the other arm rest. Our feet met in the middle and were tangled up together. I flexed my toes and they rubbed against the underside of her foot.

Katelyn burst into laughter and snatched her feet away. "Hey, stop that."

The absurdity, as well as the infection of her laughter, prompted me to do the same. "You shouldn't have such big feet then. Anyone would assume you'd be right at home in the snow, Bigfoot." I took hold of the foot I'd accidentally tickled. "My God, how big are they?"

She slapped me playfully on the shoulder. "Oh shut up, so I have big feet, they help with volleyball, ok?"

And then I looked down to my toes and then to my trainers that were positioned neatly in the space before the hearth and I blinked. "Did you take off my trainers?"

She laughed. "Yes, I didn't want you to be uncomfortable."

"Wow, I'm impressed. How did you manage that without waking me?" I plucked up my trainers and slipped them back on my feet.

"A girl learns stealth throughout her life."

That, and the fact I was totally exhausted from the last night that never was.

I checked the time on my phone. It was late afternoon – We'd been asleep several hours, doubtless making up for last night. Still no messages and still no signal. Worst of all, there was still no rumble of snow ploughs in the near distance.

"Feels like we were asleep for a while." Katelyn said as she rose to her feet, still taller than me even when I had trainers on and she didn't.

"Maybe three or four hours." I yawned and went to the kitchen. "I'm so exhausted." I filled the largest of the saucepans with snow from the other containers. It had barely commenced the melting process and needed scooping out with a wooden spoon. But at least those containers were now empty so we could forage for more snow whilst heating the contents of the large saucepan to drink in the meantime. I cursed that we didn't think to keep the rest of the snow by the fire as we slept, but it wasn't as if either of us had been in a situation like this before. We were learning survival as we went along, not that I truly believed we'd be in this puddle for much longer. Indeed, surely it could only be a matter of time before a big man on a plough shoved the snow out of the way, apologised for the inconvenience caused by the weather and enjoy the rest of your stay, I recommend the limoncello.

Suddenly I felt upbeat and turned mischievously to Katelyn. "How are you feeling? You don't strike me as the kind of girl who'd particularly enjoy the prospect of being forced to skip breakfast."

She noticed the half smile and knew I was playfully goading her. "Or lunch either, you cheeky moose." Her expression dropped a touch. "I am hungry, yes, but there are people far worse off than me out there. I can last a few hours even if my belly rumbles every few seconds."

"Well, we'll be out of here soon and somebody somewhere owes us a free meal for the inconvenience." And now my own belly rumbled at the thought of food.

Sure, I was hungry having skipped breakfast and lunch and now it was well on the way to dinner time. As athletes, we carried a higher proportion of muscle mass than most girls, which meant our bodies demanded more calories to keep everything ticking over. The entire volleyball team ate considerably more food than most girls of our age. All this meant that we'd feel hunger pangs more than most and carrying a deficiency of body fat would also mean our bodies held less reserve energy supplies in case of such an emergency as starvation. To fuel our increased need for energy, the body would first break down our muscle mass to fuel the continuation of life and shortly after, if we didn't eat, our bodies would gradually slow down the mechanisms which gave us energy, kept us alert and enabled us to think straight. Perhaps most worryingly of all, considering the freezing temperatures, our bodies would slow down their own natural ability to generate warmth. This latter point would leave us with a tough choice.

Should we keep moving to generate warmth for ourselves, which would further deplete our energy stores, or should we conserve energy by keeping still, which would contribute to further lowering our body temperatures. It was a hard choice, a catch 22, and now I looked at Katelyn and realised that if we weren't rescued, we may well have to depend on each other for survival. I still didn't think it would come to that, but it never harmed to be mentally prepared, just in case.

"We need to make our food last, Jess." She remarked whilst digging out more soft snow from the opened door.

"I know. We also need to keep the snow by the fire, kill two birds with one stone. We won't be able to keep it lit constantly, so we need to use the remaining logs for warmth and heat the water at the same time."

When we'd filled all our snow containers we closed the door, having made barely a dent in the wall of snow that prevented us from simply walking out the door and into town for a slap up meal followed by several hours on the ski runs.

It was incredible how fast the cabin temperature dropped once the logs burned themselves out. The original logs we'd ignited were now nothing but char fallen through the grate, which left us with another twenty.

"You'd think that'd be more than enough, but we should plan for the worst." I said, unsure whether or not to throw more on now or wait.

"We should light some more before going to bed and I'll melt down one of my chocolate bars for an awesome drink." She looked at me and ran her tongue slowly along her top lip.

I turned away, "Um…Then it would be a good idea to gather all our food together and take stock."

We each went to our bags and brought out what we had,

placing them on the kitchen countertop; two Galaxy bars, six sachets of hot chocolate powder and eight sachets of SoupInACup.

"Let's hope we're out of here before I need to share my SoupInACup."

Katelyn had been looking at the floor and now tilted her head back up to me. "Do...do you think everything will be ok, Jess?" And I'd thought she was the optimistic one.

I was quick to ease her fears, for myself as much as for her. "Hey, don't *you* go losing hope. Of course we'll be ok. I'm just pissed off this is eating into our skiing time." I noticed how Katelyn's eyes widened when I used the word 'our.'

"So, as long as we don't go setting up a volleyball court in here then we'll be fine, right?" Katelyn laughed nervously.

"You'd only destroy me, you genetic freak with big feet."

She hit me on the shoulder and her hand seemed to linger there a little longer than necessary, not that it was uncomfortable, just unexpected. Her smile was subtle and I had to look a little harder to know she really was smiling. It came from the inside and if anything it was her eyes that gave it away. She was a beautiful girl who despite everything was beginning to grow on me and I wanted to make sure she remained safe, at least while the universe's forces were compelling us to share the same living space. But it would feel ridiculous, after experiencing this event together, if we were to return to England and never see or speak to each other again. But I knew that would have to happen, despite the fact that right now, at this moment in time, I felt closer to her than I ever thought possible, considering our history. It really was ridiculous. But then, right now, we were all the other had. It was an abnormal situation and clearly some kind of survival instinct had kicked in, the need to work with others for the mutual good. There was no doubt in my mind, however, that pretty soon, maybe even within the next few hours, just as soon as this was over, things would return to normal and once again she'd be Katelyn the boyfriend stealing bitch, and deserved.

It was whilst rooting through the store cupboard that Katelyn found a pack of playing cards, chess set, Monopoly board and a few travel guides for the local area. Not much, but a few little things to keep us occupied did not go unwelcome.

Beneath our bedcovers, we whiled away several hours on the couch playing Gin Rummy, Blackjack and Katelyn taught me Spite and Malice, the game, not the other thing. The cold was kept sufficiently at bay and we were mostly able to remain warm, save for our hands and heads that were exposed to the room. Katelyn's ears in particular turned a rare shade of pink.

I yawned and checked my phone. "It's nine in the evening." Not that it was late, but lounging around all day in nasty temperatures with constant hunger pangs was draining.

"Looks like we're in for another night of freezing coldness." Like Katelyn, I also dreaded the forthcoming night.

"I just hope the rest of the girls are ok. It's the not knowing that's so hard."

"Knowing that lot, they'll have stuffed their bags with food, especially Marie. They'll be fine." Her confident words did not match her expression.

I rubbed my head. "Argh, food, Katelyn!"

She acknowledged my frustration by nodding her head. "I agree. Let's get this fire going and make dinner."

I took the logs with trepidation, recognising the large dent their removal made in the stack. Within minutes the logs were ignited and Katelyn held a pan containing snow and a Galaxy chocolate bar over the flame. I stirred the pot every few seconds until the snow melted and then a few minutes later, the chocolate. Then we poured the concoction into two mugs which we'd kept on the hearth to heat up. I knew from working in Starbucks that pouring hot coffee into cold cups resulted in rapidly decreasing the temperature of the coffee – We needed the heat from this drink.

Katelyn held up her mug. "To New Forest Ladies."

I hesitated then held up my own. "To surviving this bloody avalanche." I clinked the side of her cup and we sat back to enjoy dinner.

To an outsider we could have been two best friends enjoying a cup of hot chocolate by the fireplace as we sat facing each other on the couch under our respective bed covers as our feet rested entangled in the middle.

"You don't toast to the New Forest Ladies?" Katelyn asked perking an eyebrow.

I didn't owe Katelyn any explanations; I'd made my decision and that was that. But if I was ever to tell her then now would be a fitting time. "I've decided I'm quitting volleyball." I watched as her mouth gaped with that same glazed over look in the eyes. It was almost as comical as when she put her hands on her hips. I was becoming too familiar with all her mannerisms, and what's more, I found them almost comforting. "As of my last game. That's it for me."

She was shaking her head whilst trying to find some words. "Why? You're a great player." She sniffed. "Please say this isn't because of me."

"Katelyn, I'm not going to lie but I can't ever see myself pushing my way back into the team now you're back to full form. I'm not in your league as a player, not even close."

"So you're just giving up?" She looked almost cross, certainly very disappointed.

"There's no point in continuing; you're faster, taller, you have a longer reach and you're ten times more powerful. Heck, you scare the living shit out of the opposition. Most importantly of all however, Dorothy prefers you over me and she's the one who gets to decide things at New Forest Ladies."

Her eyes narrowed and she turned away to stare into the flaming logs that sizzled and hissed and glowed and emanated warmth. "Then answer me this one thing, Jessica..." she paused for effect as I awaited her question, "...what if it was Amanda, Marie or somebody else who was taking your place and not *me*. Would that change anything?"

She had me there.

And because I hesitated to answer she knew she had me too. Now that I thought about it, if it was anybody else forcing me out then I knew deep down that I'd be a team player and battle it out for my position, for the good of the team.

"Katelyn," I touched her arm, "it's because of *you*. I just can't play on the same team as you. I'm sorry, but that's the truth."

She sipped her chocolate and without thinking I did the same.

"So this is not about volleyball at all, but because of me and James." It was the first time Katelyn had mentioned his name to me, and hearing *his* name coming from *her* mouth made me suddenly very uncomfortable and I straightened against the backrest as we fell into another silence.

It was inevitable this conversation would have come up at some point, since the gods, omens, fate or whatever seemed compelled to bring us together at every possible opportunity. It was just a miracle it had been broached in the absence of kicking, screaming and hair pulling, which was something to be thankful for. I didn't believe in fate myself, but it was strange I'd ended up imprisoned with the one girl who stole my James, even though I'd tried my hardest to get away from her.

But she was right and I would not lie about it. "Well yes, obviously what you did to me has an awful lot to do with it."

She pulled her feet closer into herself and turned her body to face me. "I know I hurt you, Jess, and for what it's worth, I truly am sorry. I always thought you were a lovely girl from the first time I met you and I'm so sorry it came to this."

Our body positions were almost mirrored, except where she clasped her mug with both hands, I now drained the contents of mine. It far from satisfied my growing hunger.

"Why did you do it? I've seen how men look at you. You could have any guy you want and you chose James. Why?"

She paused for a long time and for a moment I wondered if she was struggling to come up with an answer. She pursed her wide, slender lips whilst her eyes moved between periods of remaining closed and staring into her mug. Finally she answered and her response was far from satisfying. "I guess it was a moment of weakness."

"A moment of weakness?" I yelped. "You've been dating for months." I knew she was holding something back and my instincts told me she would not divulge the answers, which annoyed me. "Tell me!"

"Jess, he just came to me. He found me that night and I was in a bad state because of my friend and..." then the tears streamed down her face and she stopped. And again, that annoyed me because she'd be sure to use the tears as an excuse not to talk about the difficult subject. It was a tactic I'd used in the past when male friends I had no sexual interest in had asked me out on a date and I hadn't wanted to upset them. It's a childish way of doing things, yes, and I'd be the first to admit I wasn't perfect. But now, as predicted, Katelyn changed tact and put it back on me. "He told me about the two of you."

My arms threw themselves up of their own accord. Just as well my drink was gone. But this was just great! There had been times, during my paranoia filled darker moments, that I imagined James was divulging our every little detail, or lack of details to Katelyn in their intimacy.

"Did Jessica give you it like that?" She'd ask, pulling herself off and collapsing abreast of him.

And he'd reply. "Jessica didn't give me it like anything."

She'd prop herself up on an elbow suddenly, her hand held over an opened mouth and a mocking expression in her eyes. "Do tell more," she'd command, her large, supple breasts still clammy and glowing after a particularly rigorous fucking. "Is Jess really as cold a fish as she appears in the changing rooms?"

And James would confirm. "Jess was as cold as that and more, but thank God I now have a girl who knows how to satisfy her man."

And I would withdraw into myself, throw everything into studying and volleyball and begin hoarding newspapers, which was strange because I never read them - But that's what James and the bitch had done to me.

Of course I knew I was being paranoid, or rather I'd assumed it, and that at least had brought me some small comfort, but now Katelyn had pretty much confirmed what had been my worst fears all along.

We never had sex! And doubtless they do it all the time – Fucking slut! And my inadequacies were not just on the volleyball court or in the changing rooms, but in other places too.

I'd been silent for a while as she watched me with a concerned expression, but now I just had to ask. "And just what did he tell you?" I feared it, but the sadomasochist within me won out.

She leaned forward with her hands clasped together. "That you're the most wonderful person he'd ever met, but that the two of you would never...you know."

There it was. I'd been right all along. Paranoia. Or was it instinct?

How did I feel about knowing my most personal affairs were being discussed by Katelyn and the man I'd dated and, I'd assumed, was falling in love with? The truth was I just didn't know. I'd have time to process it all at some other time. Was it to be expected? Maybe. But perhaps the worst part of it all was that any of it still mattered, because it shouldn't. I'd hoped I was beyond it all now and if I still cared then I didn't want to.

It was time to go into preservation mode. "Well history proves I was right never to touch that creep." And without thinking I crossed my arms and half turned away. "You're welcome to him."

She moved her hand to my arm and I recoiled without thinking. "Jess, I know what you're going through and I just want you to know that there's no reason for you to be alone in this. I've been there."

I squinted and moved away. "What are you talking about?" Was she really talking about having a boyfriend stolen, about being cheated on or something else entirely? "Spit it out woman!"

She remained silent, refusing to speak but instead appeared

to expect an answer from me. As if it was *I* who owed *her* an explanation.

"Wrong answer, bitch!" It was the first time I'd called her that and not feared being slapped. Indeed, she seemed to expect it and neither moved nor flinched. I stood, picked up my cover and laid it out on my mattress.

Five minutes later the lights were out and we were both laying faced up in our beds.

After an hour the fire burned its last.

A short time after, the shivering began and it mattered not how many layers of clothing I wore or how thick the blanket was.

In the dark silence, when you can't sleep, there's nothing to do but think and as I did I felt the tear roll down my cheek to land somewhere on the pillow to my side.

I stood, took my blanket and placed it on top of Katelyn. Her head shifted against the pillow. Then without saying a word, I pulled up one side and slid into bed beside her. I felt her arms reposition as they clasped together to rest on the top of my back. Her legs were shivering, as were mine. I lifted up my knee and using my hands, pulled her feet between my legs. The cold was a shock against my warm calves, but they soon adjusted and within seconds her toes were warm against my legs.

We fell asleep.

BUDDIES

*I*t was a deep sleep, which under the circumstances was making a statement. Not only had I slept through the bitter cold in good form, but also through Katelyn's sporadic snores. It was the latter which, into the mid-morning hours, finally woke me with a sudden recollection that the night before, to escape the cold, I'd slipped into bed next to Katelyn.

Her feet were still nestled between my legs and I could feel her hands clasped together between my shoulder blades.

The bed was warm, hot even, yet the outside, as evidenced by my freezing cold ear that poked out beyond the covers, was just that – Freezing cold. We'd turned the prospect of another agonising night, into quite the opposite, an extremely comfortable one and I had no doubt it was because of the shared warmth from our bodies.

I readjusted myself, peaking my head out from the covers to stare into the darkness and sliding my top leg across the other. It was then I felt the wetness. At first I thought it was sweat, but it was way too high to be sweat, surely? "Oh holy fuck." I mouthed silently, realising the truth that I'd leaked considerable juices during the night and now one of Katelyn's feet moved out from between my legs.

Lavender had won the battle against the earth, her more natural scent coming to the fore to defeat the brown tinted sludge from the shower.

She was awake. I knew she was because her intermittent snoring, that frequently disturbed the silence had waned and her breathing had changed rhythm. Yet her hands remained at my back and her warm foot between my legs. Both our bellies rumbled; quiet then loud, then louder and for a while it seemed like they were doing so in unison.

"Katelyn?" I whispered.

"Why are you whispering?"

I laughed. And I was so relieved to laugh because, if nothing else, it broke the tension. "I'm sorry."

"For what?"

"For getting in your bed. It was just so cold."

"Don't be silly. I'd have never slept if you hadn't crept in." She laughed, which further broke the tension.

I turned, but only halfway so I faced the ceiling, causing her foot to twist out from between my legs. "Do you think you'll have a shower today?"

"Not likely. Not without hot water, or at least clean water. Why?"

The truth was I wanted her out of the room whilst I changed. She may be fine stripping down to nothing in front of me, but there was no way I had that level of confidence, which was kind of funny, considering we'd just spent the entire night wrapped around each other. "Just wondering." Even though I felt icky and hadn't showered since England, doing so under these conditions would only serve to make me filthier than before. But this still left the problem remaining, that I couldn't see to get changed with the lights off and if I switched the lights on, then I'd be stripping down in front of Katelyn.

"I'm going to the bathroom." She said, almost as if she could read my thoughts and then she slid out of bed, turned the lights on and then I heard the bathroom door close after her.

I changed and switched on the TV, flicking immediately to the news. Katelyn returned and stood beside me, her hands clasped in at her solar plexus as we watched the reports.

Fifteen minutes past. There were stories about a local communist party politician caught in an embezzlement scandal. Of a footballer who lived locally, photographed in a nightclub with a model who wasn't his wife. And of a local fundraiser to repair an ancient church roof that'd collapsed during an earthquake. Finally, there was a segment lasting less than a minute featuring the same reporter as yesterday in Cortina d'Ampezzo. Happy locals were standing behind the woman and then it cut to the same espresso bar, the owner making a statement that he was "back to work," even if his front window was boarded up. The segment concluded by showing the snowploughs, along with their happy drivers, apparently having done their work, meandering their way along the road out of town.

"What the fuck, Katelyn?" I cried out. "Is this some kind of a sick joke? Surely they're coming to rescue us?" My fists were clenching up and my arms were actually shaking. This was no longer funny, this was now very, very serious.

"I know, honey, but don't lose hope. We both need to stay

strong." She opened up her arms and without even thinking, I swooned into them, resting my head against the front of her shoulder as I clutched my hands tight around her back. "We'll make it, don't you worry about that."

"It's just not fair." I was sobbing by this point and my tears stained the grey hoody she'd worn over another hoody. It now transpired that catching the last of the days runs was the least of our problems. In fact skiing now came far down the list when our very survival was questioned.

After a minute, I straightened, turned away and wiped the tears from my face.

A short while later, we fixed up a mug of SoupInACup. It may sound insignificant but in that moment I'd never felt further away from home, from safety, and all I'd wanted was something familiar and comforting - It worked, at least a little.

"I hope you feel honoured?" I asked, raising my mug to hers.

She touched her mug against mine. "Of course. At least now I get to see what all the fuss is about."

The energy contents were limited but it did fill a tiny part of the ever expanding hole in my stomach. The hunger was now bothering me and was progressing toward an actual pain in my belly. Though I couldn't complain because Katelyn was going through the exact same thing with surprising strength. For that, I admired her. She had backbone.

But soon after, in a joint fit of spontaneous rage and fear of the cold and of the uncertain, we ransacked the cabin for anything practical that would burn. Picture frames, a wooden shelf, books, even a sculpture; we threw them all to the flames. They would do for the time being, not only to keep us warm but to slake our anger.

Then we regained clarity as well as level heads and the natural instinct for survival as we realised that just like the wood that diminished depressingly fast before our eyes, the cabin perishables would also have to be rationed.

We occupied much of the day gathering things we could potentially burn. I had my eye on the beams that supported the ceiling. Unfortunately I had no idea how, nor the means with which to hack them down. Fortunately, the bed frames were made from wood and since we'd only be using Katelyn's from now on, my bed was expendable as was the mattress. We gathered towels, spare clothes, sheets, even the ironing board cover would be sure to take to flame. During our sacking, we happened across a box of candles; always welcome in a situation where our utilities were practically non-existent. It may only be a matter of time before the power went the same way as the gas and water; the same way *hope* was also heading.

Then evening was upon us once more and we faced another night of uncertainty. Long silences dragged out as we drank our evening hot chocolate, melted from the last remaining Galaxy bar.

I remembered once reading how the only reason our European ancestors had survived the Ice Age was because they'd stockpiled and then rationed enough food to last the winter. Those who didn't, or those who raided the pantry whenever they felt like it, would have starved to death, ensuring their lineage was not passed on. The advantage they had, though, was knowing the winter would eventually turn to spring and food would be abundant once more. They could plan whereas we never had the opportunity. I feared, assuming we would eventually be rescued, that we'd already consumed too much of our scarce resources. The problem now was not knowing when, if ever, our rescue would come. But then this is what long hours of inactivity does to your mind - There is very little to do but think and much of your thoughts are negative. It was odd, but Katelyn was the only thing keeping me sane.

The fire flared and crackled, the smoke darker than before, the varnish from the broken wooden chair made snapping noises and omitted an odour. A row of pans, bowls and other assorted containers lay on the hearth; each full with newly warmed water. The lights were out and a line of candles flickered from the mantelpiece. Hey, despite everything, we were still on holiday.

"Hard day." Katelyn stated as fact, looking quite worn out.

"Sure was." I felt it myself. Ripping apart mattresses and furniture, despite being fun was also hard work and utilised energy we didn't have to spare. My belly growled, which in turn set off Katelyn's.

"What do you miss the most?" She asked.

That was an easy one. "Food! When you don't have it, God, do you ever crave it." I ran a hand through my hair which had become dull and dirty. "More specifically; chicken salad, tuna salad, jacket potato and not having to ration SoupInACups."

"I'll tell you what I miss...hot showers."

"Ah, yes, I would have to agree with you there, but hot showers are luxuries, whereas food is a necessity."

"Agreed. It's not exactly a fair contest, but showers..." She drawled the word out and ran her hands through her hair just as I had seconds before, then over her face. "I am so sticky, I cannot tell you." Her eyes moved and fixed upon the water heating by the fire as she spent a few seconds pinching her bottom lip. "Sod it!" She leapt up from the couch and began delving into her bag.

"Katelyn, what are you doing?" I asked with alarm.

She returned with a pink face cloth in her hand and a grin on her face. "Jess, I'm a nice clean girl at heart and I refuse to live like this any longer." She unzipped her jacket and cast it to the couch, quickly followed by two hoodies and, quite bizarrely, her New Forest Ladies playing jersey.

Lavender was vaguely detectable, not that I was paying any attention to *that* in the moment, as my heart raced so fast it almost hurt. I may have gasped or squealed something unfathomable, but if I did I couldn't be sure. My God, but she was stripping, right in front of me...Me! I felt the urgent need to turn my head, to stare into the safety of the wall, but I just couldn't and besides, to do so would be to actively ignore it, which would only make the situation even tenser, because let's face it, there was no hiding from the fact she was right now standing before me in her bra, two large breasts stretching the fabric to bursting point. And now she was unbuttoning her jeans and then she began slowly working them down her legs, which took quite some effort because they were an extremely tight fit around her athletically muscular thighs. They bunched at the floor and she lifted her foot and tugged them off before throwing them the same way as the rest of her discarded garments and after that there wasn't a great deal left.

I exhaled as I watched her straighten and turn to face the fire, its glow shimmering on her tanned skin. She had supremely long legs, sculpted and muscular. Her buttocks were hard and pert, her skin tight, the ass of an athlete and my eyes became lost on her black lacy underwear, the back of which had slipped up between her cheeks.

She bent slowly over to pick up the larger saucepan, placed it on the ledge and submerged the cloth in the water as I was made suddenly aware, by a tapping sound emanating from my foot against the wooden floor, that my entire leg was shaking. If she noticed then she was too polite to make any indication as she rang out the cloth, the sinews showing in her arms and then, almost like it was nothing, began rubbing the cloth over her neck and shoulders. Her eyes were closed and she was humming something melodic before returning to the pan, soaking the rag once more and glancing it over her sternum from where faint wisps of steam rose, or it may have been my imagination. "Hmm, the water's so nice."

"Huh?" I blurted out at a volume that sounded incredibly loud to my ears. My mouth was so dry and I swallowed, making another loud noise she had to have heard.

She reached up, bent her arm back and attempted to clean the area between her shoulders, her bicep noticeably popping as she did and then she juddered and winced. "Ouch, damn it...my shoulder." She turned around to face me and looked down with a pretty please expression, her shoulders and sternum glistening with moisture, her breasts looming in my line of sight and she held out the cloth in an arm half extended in my direction, to where I was sitting almost in a daze. "Jess, you couldn't help me out here, could you?"

"What?" Something ricocheted in my chest and I swallowed again, harder this time. "You want me to give you a...um... sponge...cloth bath...um, wipe?"

She bounced once on her toes and looked mischievous. "Hmm, I guess that's what it is. I don't think I can do it on my own, I'm just not flexible enough." She looked at me with puppy dog eyes and her bottom lip was sticking out. "I'm just so clammy, Jess, and I hate it so much." She didn't make it sound like such a big deal, which made it a little less weird, even though I was profoundly aware that it probably was. The truth is my head was spinning with all kinds of strange shit, chemicals I suppose, and those things surging around in your bloodstream can make you think and do stuff in the heat of the moment you wouldn't ordinarily even contemplate, or so I thought.

I cleared my throat and could barely believe the words once they were spoken. "Um, yeah, fine I guess." I stood and almost lost my footing, then held out my hand and she gave me the cloth.

She turned away, which made it easier, and began humming again as I submerged the rag in the pan, the water a pleasant warm on my skin, before wringing it out.

I hesitated a beat and wasn't sure why, probably just getting my head round the strange turn of events. I'd never washed anyone other than myself before but there was nothing sexual or depraved in it, we all needed to bathe and under the circumstances there was no better way of doing it. Indeed, Katelyn in her confidence had made it a complete non-issue and the only way it would now become one would be if I, in my typical stuffiness, made it so. Better just get on with it and then when it was all over we could carry on like nothing happened.

So, I pressed the cloth against her back and rubbing it gently up and down, I began to wash Katelyn. Her flesh was smooth and clear with thick musculature beneath, built from a lifetime of playing sports. When I reached her bra strap, I lifted it away with a finger and cleaned beneath, taking care not to miss an inch. I moved to the gentle arch of her lower back and then to the generously proportioned curvature of her buttocks, which were exposed due to the scarcity of her underwear and I marvelled at how they barely moved as I ran the cloth over her. Was she clenching? – No of course not – Why would she do that? Then I had to crouch as I worked down the length of her legs, requiring several replenishes from the pan as I did, the impressive muscles in her thighs and calves hard beneath my fingertips. I took care of her, like a mother would her child, ensuring she was clean all over, then I paid extra attention to her feet and toes and at one point she giggled, which further eased the tension, not that there was very much by this point.

I finished with her back and she could now easily wash her own front, but instead, I simply stood and she turned around to face me, her look suggesting there'd be no issue with my continuing. Clearly she was enjoying the experience, sort of like getting a massage, or so I assumed, and it wasn't altogether unpleasant for me. On the contrary, it felt like I was getting closer to a girl who was, despite all the crap, becoming a friend and I was surprised at how little negative undercurrents I felt myself, despite having always considered myself a prude despite my youth. There was something quite primal about it and if people didn't typically wash like this anymore, it was a shame, because back in the day surely they would have before the invention of showers. I rinsed out the cloth again and we stood toe to toe as I cleaned her shoulder from the front and down her arm, then the other side. I was gentle over her sternum, even though she'd already covered around there, and then I neared her breasts, her deep cleavage mere inches from my fingers as I dabbed at the flesh around that area and averted my eyes, cleared my throat a little and, having gone as far as decently possible, forgetting for a moment the obstacle she was still wearing, I nodded, job done, and was about to return the cloth to the pan when...

"...Oh, one second," she said in sudden realisation and turned around. "My bra...you'll have to do it." The words weren't an order, or a request even, but more an assumption, like it was totally logical I'd have to unclasp her bra myself before continuing to wash her.

I swallowed and felt my leg shake again. When this had started I hadn't thought cleansing her would go quite *this* far but again, there was no awkwardness in it; tension, absolutely, but no awkwardness, which surprised the heck out of me and I didn't know how she was doing it. It wasn't like there was any alcohol involved either, just this surreal moment that should have been borderline distressing for me, but wasn't. Instead it was strangely captivating. And that's why I didn't think much to it as I unhooked her black lace bra and allowed it to fall to the floor.

And that's when everything changed.

She slowly turned around. God. And there they were. And my vision blurred as my pupils dilated and refocused and for a second there was lightheadedness and I had to swallow again because I'd never known my mouth so dry.

Her breasts had barely needed the bra support at all – Despite being large – Um, very large, yes, and round. How could they appear so firm? I mean, I'd seen them before, for the odd stolen second, but not this close and in the absence of showers and steam they appeared just as I remembered them, yet different too, and that I could not explain, not that it even mattered and I was thinking gibberish now because that's what these two large globes had done to me.

"Jess?" She startled me. "Are you ok?" She'd been watching me the whole time, unlike for the vast majority of this, um, whatever we were doing, and I wasn't sure if she'd wanted to see my reaction or not.

"Um, yes. Sorry...sponge bath." I glanced over to the pan, experienced a strange limbo moment upon seeing the cloth wasn't there and then realised I was still holding it. Get a grip Jess.

And where there'd been a surprising lack of tension before, I sure felt it now, even if it was all in my head. In fact it was unbearable, like the revealing of her boobs had flicked a switch inside my head. And where before I'd always found it hard to make small talk with Katelyn, now I was finding it borderline impossible. Now I felt a greater need than ever to fill the tense silences with meaningless words as I grasped the cloth before this Goddess, but no words materialised. Oh, Katelyn, but why couldn't *you* say something to fill the silences? Or perhaps she could see my discomfort and was secretly enjoying it - The crap that flies around my head in such moments.

I brought the cloth to beneath her breast and cupped the globe where it met her ribcage. My hand was full and weighty as my whole arm trembled and there was not one thing I could do to stop it. She had to know my arm was shaking and that I was petrified, but if she did, she was good enough to make no indication. Instead she closed her eyes once more and continued humming some lullaby I recognised from childhood. I gently pressed and stroked the lower portion of her breast that nestled against her ribcage, unable to take my eyes off her areola, that was small, as I worked towards her nipple, that was large and stood hard and tipped from the warm water in the cabin chill. I slowly progressed to the upper portion, tenderly bathing her and I wondered if I'd spent longer on this one breast than on all the rest of her combined.

"You're embarrassed about being undressed in front of the

girls aren't you?" She finally broke the tension, only to create some more.

"What? Um, maybe a little bit...I don't know...not really." I answered immediately with a hardly thought out response.

She giggled and I wasn't sure if it was due to my reply or because I'd moved the cloth back down to her nipple. "I think you are. Don't think I haven't noticed how you conceal yourself." She giggled again. "It's very sweet. But trust me, we've all seen you naked and you have absolutely nothing to be embarrassed about."

"What? You've seen me naked?" My voice came out faint and I wondered if my skin had turned a shade whiter.

"Many times. You have a beautiful body, Jess, certainly no reason to feel pressured to dress in the dark or after all the other girls have left the changing rooms." She rubbed my arm and tilted her head. "It's funny and it's cute...your mannerisms."

I giggled myself, partly in embarrassment and I knew my cheeks were flushing. I thought about Katelyn's many mannerisms I'd started picking up on and how I found them truly endearing, even if I only ever saw them when I was angry with her. "Thank you. I suppose it's hard being around so many athletic women, you kind of feel inferior. I suppose it's natural in a way, you know, getting embarrassed." I moved to her other breast, not knowing how much time I'd spent on the first. The candlelight flicked and shimmered against her skin.

"Well you're not embarrassed now, are you? In fact, if I didn't know any better, I'd swear you were enjoying this." She spoke with an obvious swagger and I knew she was joking, but still...

"Well, I can't say I've ever done this to another girl before but at least it's not me who's the naked one here." It was a great relief to be talking and joking and I moved down to her abdomen, the faintest sign of hard abdominals every time she exhaled. This girl truly was in fantastic shape.

"Me neither, but I can't tell you how incredible it feels, not just being bathed by a nice warm cloth, but having the feeling of being clean again."

I'd crouched down to get a better angle on her abdomen and was paying particular attention to the line that ran down the centre when I answered almost nonchalantly. "Oh, Katelyn, stop it, you're making me jealous." I glanced up and saw the wide suggestive grin and that was when the cloth fell from my slackened grasp. If she was thinking what I thought she was then she could forget it. Talk about a mismatch. No way was I getting naked in front of *this* girl.

I retrieved the cloth and began scrubbing the side of her thigh, going over old ground because everything else was done and she had to forget that last suggestion, myself too, even if I couldn't.

"Ooh, one sec...you're forgetting something." And then she absolutely inserted her thumbs inside the elastic of her black lace underwear.

My heart leapt into my mouth as I almost lost my balance and tumbled to the side, the proximity of the couch the only thing stopping me from doing so. "No, Katelyn, there's really no need, I can wash around..."

...But it was too late. She'd pulled them down her legs with a practiced speed and I watched as they were flung across my vision to land expertly on her playing jersey that was sagged over the backrest. "I'm really not sure black's my colour, what do you think?"

What?

"Um red, or black...yes, black is fine." I stuttered over the words, still staring aghast at the little black things perched atop the couch, whilst mentally preparing myself for what was coming.

She ran her hands through her hair, which to me still looked as shiny as it had at the restaurant. "I suppose my hair can wait, we'll need more water for that job." What was she saying? Her hair now? Was it all really so elementary to her?

But there was no getting away from it, and so I breathed, turned my head and beheld the sight of her pussy.

My immediate thought was that she was smooth, perfectly smooth in fact, like she'd shaved only today. But why would she have and for what purpose? Was she expecting a visit from her boyfriend or something? I was still in a crouched position, not easy to maintain when your legs are turning to jelly, and my eyes were more or less level with her most intimate body part. And still she displayed not the slightest hint of reserve.

"I can't tell you how good it feels not having to shower in cold brown water. It's no way to live, Jess. Makes me wonder for how many thousands of years people have been walking around so dirty." Is what I think she said, not that the actual words were relevant but that she was speaking at all, just another day in Katelyn's world.

She was wet, very wet, and for a moment I wondered if water had run down her body and collected there, but I dismissed that silly thought almost immediately. It was now I realised I'd been biting my lower lip, whatever that meant, and I could taste the slightest hint of blood on my palate. I raised the cloth, hesitated a beat then lightly brushed it over her outer lips. She juddered but made no issue of it, like *this* was the most natural thing in the world. Oh, I was aware of what was happening, I think, but couldn't be sure I wouldn't wake at any moment in that freezing cold bed, or maybe even back in England. It was all so bizarre, I thought, as I brought the cloth away, the tiniest stream of thin transparent juice clinging to her before breaking. Then I cleaned delicately around her opening and along her clit, her faint shudders that came from the pit of her belly resonating on my fingertips – She was enjoying this and again I found myself wondering how much my discomfort was a part of it. But then, I couldn't be completely sure I wasn't enjoying it myself, even now, after this ridiculous escalation.

"Hmm...there's a certain appeal to going caveman...hmm." Her breathing was deeper than before and her breasts heaved with every inhalation.

"Yes, if I had a time machine..." Meaningless words and I trailed off uselessly. If my arm had been shaking before, now it was all but pulsating. With my inferiority complex, I should have been horrified by the mere thought of washing Katelyn's sex bits, but I just couldn't bring myself to stop, at least not until I knew she was clean, and why *that* detail was so important I couldn't say. It was strangely erotic, yet at the same time it wasn't. It was like she needed help and only *I* could take care of her. It was a duty. And in its own way it was especially beautiful because only hours earlier I had truly despised this girl. But now?

Something had happened and was continuing to happen. But whether I was changing or natural disasters brought out deep lying emotions within people that they never knew existed, I didn't know. Either way, I'd now completed the task and the, um, somewhat different experience was over and now things could go back to normal.

I used my free hand to steady myself and pushed up from the floor. "Um, I think I'm about done." My thighs ached yet I'd barely noticed the fatigue that had long since set in and it felt good to stand again. I returned the cloth to the saucepan and wiped my hands over my jacket. It was odd being so well wrapped up in layer after layer of warm clothing whilst Katelyn was standing bare before me, still, I gave her breasts one last appraisal as I turned away and set off toward the bed that I could almost hear calling my name.

I felt the hand on my shoulder.

"And where do you think you're going?"

I pointed to the bed and gave her an expression as if to suggest she'd gone daft. "Where do you think?"

"Jess, it wouldn't be very fair, after you just spent fifteen minutes giving me a sponge bath, if I didn't at least return the favour." She lunged closer, grabbed ahold of me by the jacket zipper and began pulling me back toward the hearth, to where the flames still spat and roared and made pretty patterns but this wouldn't be pretty, not by a long way.

"Oh, no, Katelyn, don't worry about it." After what I'd already experienced this night, I really needed to lie down.

"Don't be silly, Jess." And there was a naked girl unzipping me and when that was done she was tugging at the sleeves of my thick ski jacket. "You know, I really don't fancy sharing such a small cabin with a girl who smells."

"Oh, no, it's really not that small, is it?" I laughed and tried to object but I knew my protests were half-hearted and almost comical and I feared why that might be. Did I want this? Did I want her to stop? Would I be disappointed if she did? I wasn't even drunk, yet I was under the influence of something. "Please, Katelyn," her name came out quite high pitched and I knew I was at her mercy yet I had to resist this somehow, at least in a token way, "well I suppose I can clean myself. Would that be all right? Unlike you, I don't have a shoulder injury so..."

She yanked the sleeves off my arms and then discarded the jacket as though it was some major inconvenience. "Nonsense, I've seen you stretching and you're even less flexible than I am, you'll never get those hard to reach spots."

"Oh, I will, I promise, I'm very flexible. Let me just take the warm water to the bathroom and I'll make a start on myself, shall I?"

She must have been encouraged by my tone because she wasted no time with my sweaters, pulling three layers over my head in one go. My vision flashed black as the material flicked over my eyes and then it was light again and Katelyn was dumping the hindrance to the floor and then I was standing, terrified yet aroused, in only my bra.

"Jess, you'll freeze in that bloody room. I'm seriously not taking *no* for an answer." She raised her voice and was all seriousness like a school teacher with narrowed eyes - She'd see me naked yet.

What else could I do but submit?

She clasped her hand around my wrist, probably out of fear I'd run to the bathroom and lock myself in there, then I was shocked suddenly when, as quick as I'd come to expect from this girl on the volleyball court, she reached around my back with both arms, crushing our breasts together. It was a unique sensation, soft yet animalistic which sent a lightning bolt shooting down my spine and I knew she felt it too because her lips parted slightly and her eyes widened even as they remained fixed on mine. I could feel her fingers fiddling with my bra clasp and then I felt the release of tension up front as my bra fell to the floor between our toes - In all, about two seconds - She'd done this before.

"Right, now we're getting somewhere." She stepped back, hands on hips, and I thought I detected a subtle smile as her eyes flicked briefly downwards.

Instinctively, I crossed my arms over my breasts but one stern look from Katelyn was all it took and I allowed them to flop uselessly down by my sides.

What could I do? In one fell swoop the band aid had been ripped off. And it no longer mattered because now she had seen them and that could never again be reversed. I felt a slight chill on my flesh, still adjusting to being exposed in such a way, but I wasn't about to go running to the bathroom, even if I wanted to, which I didn't.

"See, that's not too bad is it? All that fuss..." she rolled her eyes for my benefit then looked down at my jeans.

"Oh no, Katelyn." What had possessed this girl?

She shook her head. "Jess, you know this is going to happen whether you cooperate or not." I knew this naked girl was serious, which was terrifying, yet for whatever reason exhilarating at the same time. What had this avalanche done to us?

"No, Katelyn, please. You have my top half, ain't that enough?" But I knew my verbal objections in no way matched my body language, which only encouraged her further.

"Nice try, missy." And her fingers were fiddling with the button on my jeans, and that was followed by the distinctive sound of my zipper being pulled down.

Then, feeling the last of my resistance dissolving, she squatted and used both hands to tug down the barrier and then my jeans were discarded unceremoniously behind her. She stood and then the urgency and games and confusion and everything else of before ceased.

She slid her thumbs inside my underwear's elastic and locked onto my eyes with hers, as though silently asking for permission. My heart pounded heavier than I'd ever known before but my curiosity had become so overwhelming I just had to experience this. And she must have read my mind because then she slowly moved downwards, all the way her eyes remaining level with the garment as they slipped down my legs. When they reached the floor I stepped out from them and she placed them, quite carefully, on the couch next to her own clothes.

She stood, I trembled, she whispered, "turn around."

I obeyed and then felt the warm cloth over my shoulders. Without realising, my arms again gravitated to my breasts in a self-protective embrace, not that it would make a difference because Katelyn would demand access very soon regardless.

She moved onto my back, all the time making small, delicate strokes and it felt wonderful. "See, this isn't so bad is it." Then I felt warm moisture on my buttocks as she brushed over my soft flesh. "You really have no reason to be so shy about your body. For heaven's sake, you're an athlete. You have no flabby bits, no cellulite, not even a dimple. I don't know how you do it."

There was silence for a while as she moved down to my legs and I felt compelled to say something. "I guess...just being around you...and some of the others..." I allowed it to trail off, having made my point.

She sighed as the cloth worked the inside of my thigh. "Well, you really do have a great body."

I watched her intently, for several minutes, as she cleaned the backs of my legs, then moved round to the front. She hummed, as though she was carrying out some mundane household chore, as though this was a normal thing for her. For me, I had simply given up trying to rationalise just what had happened this night – It was what it was – I was standing completely naked, receiving a sponge bath from a beautiful girl, who was also completely naked, in a small log cabin, a blazing log fire and flickering candlelight after an avalanche in Italy. And even though I felt woozy, I was completely sober.

And then I was wrenched out from my thoughts as the damp cloth grazed my pussy. I had been wet, I knew that much, and if Katelyn had seen just how wet she'd made me with her gentle caresses then she made no issue of it. And strangely, as my body shuddered once more, I felt immersed and completely comfortable with having Katelyn touch my most sensitive and intimate of areas. Why had I been so nervous before? This was the most natural and beautiful thing in the world.

She stood as she worked her way up from my midriff. And then she was on my breast. She was so gentle and caring, I watched her face as she intently cleaned every inch of my sphere. Unlike my own, her hands were calm and completely under control.

She looked into my eyes and spoke softly, "I don't think you'll be so afraid of me anymore, Jess. You've seen every inch of my body and I've seen every inch of yours." Her lips curled up at each side, the candlelight shimmered on her breasts, much larger than mine, as they hovered irresistibly close to touching my own.

The tension was incredible and there was a need for me to say something, anything, but I couldn't think of any words and doubted they'd come out coherent anyway. The cloth dropped to the floor and Katelyn grazed her fingertips down the outsides of my arms, I shivered and smiled and she linked my fingers in hers and looked straight into my eyes.

Was this really happening?

She tilted forwards and my breasts pressed against hers. I knew what was coming and I surrendered myself to the possibility of it. I leaned into her and our thighs made contact. Our lips were an inch apart and she ran her tongue along them in preparation and without knowing, I did the same.

"Jess." She whispered.

"Katelyn." I closed my eyes.

Our lips connected and as they did she made a high pitched hum. I squeezed her hands lightly and in return she squeezed them harder. She pressed forward with her hips as her tongue entered my mouth, joining with my own and together they danced a tender rhythm. She was so gentle and I lost myself to the sensation of kissing another girl.

But that's exactly what Katelyn was – A girl. And everything had happened so fast and I panicked.

I broke away. "I'm so sorry, Katelyn. Please forgive me. I never meant to..."

"Jess? What's the matter?" There was alarm in her voice, her shoulders drooped, her brows furrowed and I hated that *I'd* done that.

I gathered up my clothes as quickly as possible and rushed to the bathroom, locking the door behind me.

WHEN I LEFT THE BATHROOM SHE WAS ALREADY LYING IN BED, facing the other way, a solitary candle illuminating the immediate area. I'd used the time to dress for the night and brush my teeth, not to mention throw cold water over my pussy, that still throbbed in excruciating frustration. It did nothing to allay my needs. Oh, how I ached and regretted terribly not thinking to pleasure myself while I was in there, but to do so, whilst thinking of her, would be to acknowledge my sexual attraction for another girl. Nonetheless, I felt ready to explode because the tension down below was unbearable.

"Excuse me." I lifted up the covers at my end of the bed. It was times like these I regretted the fact my own bed now existed only as CO_2 drifting over the Italian Dolomites.

Katelyn shuffled as far over as the space would allow and then we were plunged into darkness as she blew out the candle. "Goodnight, Jess."

Unlike the night before, there'd be no physical contact between us this night and over the next half hour or so, all I heard was the occasional sniff coming from Katelyn, not her cute customary half snores, which was evidence she lay awake, as did I.

In fact, I doubted very much I'd experience much sleep tonight. Certainly not like the night before, which had been so wonderful, deep and trouble free.

But God, how my pussy ached.

It took a lot to turn me on. It was probably the reason I was still a virgin. Few men had the ability to sexually excite me and none that I'd met so far had ever succeeded in taking me to bed because I'd wanted nothing else other than to fuck them.

But Katelyn...

...Katelyn had done something to me. She had awakened something that sat deep within my core, deep down in my soul and this new experience, these new feelings, for another woman, who only a few days ago I'd despised, truly terrified me.

And now that this evening was over, I could see where my heart and mind and soul were with the addition of some clarity.

But I needed time to allow it to sink in and I wanted to be sure there were true feelings there and that it wasn't temporary insanity, brought on by our confines. Perhaps I was wrong and next week I'd return to the comfort of being depressed over James and I'd laugh and cringe from the memory of what had occurred tonight and what else could have occurred if I hadn't stopped it. But if that didn't happen, what then?

After a while, I heard a sound, quiet and rhythmic. What was it? I held my breath in an attempt to decipher the strange yet soft sound, which came seemingly from Katelyn. It picked up, increased its pace and was accompanied by intermittent squeaks from the bed springs.

The breath caught in my chest as I pretended to sleep for clearly, Katelyn thought I was in my slumber. My pussy ached like never before, the urge to reach down and touch myself, so powerful. But I just couldn't. I couldn't risk Katelyn knowing what I was doing, that I was touching myself with images of her breasts and arse and legs and hair and everything else flooding my mind.

Her breathing increased in volume and I felt the covers twitching as her fingers went to work. Her leg swept across the bed and there was a low groan.

My hand hovered over my belly and I wanted, needed, dearly, to move down, to touch myself, to satisfy myself, just as Katelyn was doing. It was sheer torture, but somehow I managed to stop my hand from sliding down to that area between my legs, where I knew I'd find an ocean of wetness.

The movements increased further in speed and then her other hand moved higher up, I assumed to cover her mouth, as she attempted to overpower the sounds that tried to escape.

There was a suppressed whimper and she shuddered for longer than I ever thought possible from a euphoric climax.

I lay numb for what seemed like forever, silent and still as possible until finally Katelyn turned over and then she too remained in silence.

I never heard the snores and it was a long time until I drifted off to sleep.

FADING

I woke up shivering, my feet especially felt the chill despite the thermal socks I'd donned overnight. I wasn't going to lie; I'd missed the body heat shared with Katelyn the night before, her feet tangled up with mine and her sweet breaths warming the back of my neck.

Still no snores? How was that possible?

"Katelyn?"

No response.

I moved my foot over to her side of the bed. She wasn't there. Not only that but the sheets were cold. My heart skipped a beat.

I leapt from the bed and flicked on the light switch. Katelyn wasn't in the main room, but the bathroom door was closed. Relief flooded through me, not that she could disappear anywhere, but still...

Then I heard the pattering of water. Was she seriously in the shower? Why on earth would she do that unless she possessed the desire to smell like mud for the rest of the day?

I approached the door and knocked. "Katelyn, are you ok in there?"

No answer was forthcoming but the water did shut off in response, followed a short time after by feet hitting the floor. I pictured her stepping out from the bath tub, water dripping from those same curves that only hours earlier I'd been tenderly cleaning - And this morning she'd opted for a shower. Not just a shower, but a freezing cold shower with filthy water. I couldn't help but feel spurned. Was all this because I'd rejected her last night?

The door opened, Katelyn breezed past and not only did she forego making eye-contact, but unusually for her leaving the bathroom, she was fully clothed.

"Good morning, Katelyn." I said almost as a question.

She was heading toward the kitchen at the far end of the cabin and continued for another three paces before finally stopping and turning slowly around. "Oh, hey. Good morning, you."

Well, that certainly came as a relief. At least she was talking to me. "I'll just go ahead and brush my teeth and then we'll get the fire started for breakfast." The mere mention of the word opened up a chorus of rumbling complaints from my belly. How I wished breakfast could consist of more than a sachet of soup.

Katelyn blinked and changed direction, walking instead toward the hearth where she grabbed her bag before sauntering in the direction of the door. "Oh, don't worry about it, I'll just get something in town." She absolutely said like she really was about to head out.

And then I watched almost dumbstruck as she pressed down

on the handle, found it was locked, fumbled through her jacket pocket, brought out the key, unlocked the door and opened it before finding herself blocked by a wall of snow and ice.

"Um, Katelyn?"

She turned slowly around to face me and slapped her forehead. "Oh, you must think I've gone totally mad?"

"Are you sure you're ok?"

She dropped her bag, walked over to the other side of the cabin and instead gathered up the last of the remaining logs before setting them into the fireplace. "Yep, other than the cold and hunger. Soups up?"

"Of course." I said relieved and took two sachets of SoupInACup along with the usual pan filled with snow. A few minutes later we drank our less than meagre breakfast and watched the local news. More stories of corrupt politicians and wayward footballers, which hardly came as a surprise.

We stock checked our consumables, which was thoroughly depressing. Our fuel would run out before our so called food, though not by much. Obviously without fuel with which to heat the snow for the food then the sachets of soup and chocolate would be worthless anyway, so we made the decision to halve our fuel rations which, because our supply was so low, would only prolong it one more day. By the end of tomorrow, we'd have no food and no fuel.

"We may have to consider doing something drastic." I said as we both sat by the fire. "If they were going to rescue us then it should have happened by now."

"Drastic like what?"

"I don't know...think!" I glared into the fire, the smoke escaping up the chimney and pointed. "That's way too narrow for either of us to fit through, even on this enforced diet." I didn't think I'd lost a dress size, yet.

"I'm thinking we could just set fire to the place, melt the snow around us and simply walk out." She looked serious, which was the scary thing.

"Um, last resort, Katelyn."

She'd positioned herself a little further away than usual. So she was upset with me, I could understand that. I had rejected her and now she was distancing herself from me, but I'd be lying if I said it didn't sting. At one point I found myself shuffling a little closer, which I didn't think she noticed.

"We could scoop our way out with the saucepan." She said with way too much enthusiasm but I knew she was being sarcastic.

"It may be our only viable option." I regarded her adorable face, those chiselled cheekbones and green eyes, her cute little nose and hair that perfectly framed her features. I wanted to protect her, even though I needed protecting myself. We only had each other, a fact that was now starker than ever before. "But we must stay strong, honey." I reached over and touched her hand which, despite being close to our source of heat, was cold.

She pulled away at a speed that took me by surprise. "I *am* staying strong. Don't worry about me." Her voice was cheerful and upbeat, masking the previous gesture.

The day passed us by and to my growing sadness we spent hour after hour at separate sides of the cabin, in silence, just like the first day in here, occupying our time however we could. I retrieved my physiotherapy books and made a start revising the mechanics of the shoulder joint. It didn't take long before a sudden guilty realisation washed over me, that I'd only brought the damn books in order to ignore Katelyn. It was as though deep down I knew I'd somehow be stuck with her and now we were ignoring each other I hated it. Katelyn, meanwhile, occupied herself by pottering aimlessly about the cabin, spending long moments in silence out from my company.

And then we were plunged into darkness.

A SCRATCHING SOUND EMANATED FROM THE BATHROOM, which had to have been Katelyn scrabbling around in the dark for the door handle.

The power had gone. Under the circumstances it was probably a blessing it had lasted as long as it did, considering the lack of gas, water, food and heat. In fact we'd only used the electricity for the news bulletins and lighting. The former was truly depressing anyway and only served to sap our hope, while thankfully we'd already located an abundance of candles to substitute for the latter.

Using the light from my phone, Katelyn and I lit several candles, placing them at intervals around the cabin. The end result was adequate light in the form of a serene glow. For thousands of years humans would have used candles for this very purpose so we were hardly put out by it.

Regardless, after a few extra minutes of attempted studying with squinted eyes, I gave up and decided to go to bed. "I'm turning in for the night, Katelyn." Now my belly was truly howling and caused no small amount of pain and I knew I'd experience difficulties tonight.

"Sure, I'll be with you soon." She said, from her supine position on the couch where I assumed she was reading a book on her phone's Kindle app.

A short time later I was roused by a crash and I sprang from the bed to hurry over to Katelyn who was standing over a pan she'd evidently dropped on the floor. A thick sludge had spread over the floorboards, in the middle of which was Katelyn.

"What happened? Are you ok?"

She was squinting but didn't look up. "Sorry if I woke you. I was just heating some water and the damn thing slipped out of my hand."

I reassured her that everything was ok and heated some water for her, which she then drank. Then we headed to bed – Another night at separate sides.

The next morning, candles still illuminated the room but there was something different, something that filled my heart with optimism.

A slim beam of light was shining in through one of the windows. Was the snow melting or had the wind simply blown away the top layer? Or perhaps the snow was never as high as we'd originally thought.

During the night Katelyn had turned to face me and in the small brightness the morning had brought I spent unknown minutes watching her as she slept. Her beautiful tanned skin and long brown hair, glossy even now, perfect features at peace with life, intermittent semi-snores as her eyelids flickered. I sighed and dragged my carcass out from under the covers.

An hour after I had risen Katelyn was still wrapped up snug and I decided not to wake her since she looked so peaceful. An hour after that I glanced over again to find her awake.

"Hey, morning. It's time for breakfast, sleepy head." We were down to our last sachet of soup each. After this final meal and the hot chocolate powder, we would starve.

Her words were monotone. "Jess, I don't think I can make

the game today." Well, she'd finally succeeded in warping my mind.

My eyebrows dipped and I crossed the floor to hear her better. "What? What game?"

"Worthing DC...Or is it VC?"

I pressed the backs of my fingers to her forehead. Shit. She was cold. "Katelyn, we play VC *next* week. We're in Italy."

"Oh, yes, of course, I know that, but I'm afraid it's still too cold to play today. I won't be much good. You take my place. I never wanted to take your place. So you can have it."

My heart thumped. It was like finding out your best friend had turned senile – In fact yes, it was exactly like that.

I was no doctor and I couldn't get any internet signal on my phone to check her symptoms. But as part of my physiotherapy course, we had touched lightly upon a range of conditions that could afflict our patients. I doubted the lack of food, that hunger would cause anyone to suffer from confusion, at least not after this short period of time.

The obvious conclusion was that the cold had affected her; a combination of cold air and freezing showers, doubtless exacerbated by a reduction in food intake, which would further prevent her body from generating warmth through natural processes and I feared she was in the early stages of hypothermia.

I stroked her hair and heard my voice nearly break. "Don't you worry about taking my place. I just want you to be the best player you can be." I took ahold of her hand, which was equally like ice and my thoughts were that her blood was retreating from her skin's surface in order to protect vital organs. "But right now, we're in Italy and we're going skiing." My words came out with a tremor and I had to turn away to suppress my stinging eyes and breathe.

Then I saw the realisation in her eyes and she closed them with a smile and then opened them again. "Of course, skiing, Jess. But I can't go today, I'm a little too cold for it."

I told her to stay in bed and ensured her double socked feet were fully enveloped in the covers.

Forgetting about myself, I made her some soup and sat with her as she drank it. We spoke about England and volleyball and thankfully it was like talking to the Katelyn I'd become accustomed to and she seemed truly embarrassed about earlier. "You must think I'm such a moose." She said, blushing.

But I wasn't taking any chances, not with this girl, not now. It was funny how under such pressure, when you'd expect your brain to scramble, that you actually come up with some of your best ideas. That was when I emptied out the mustard bottle and filled it with freshly boiled water to create an effective hot water bottle which, after Katelyn had drifted off, I pushed against her belly.

I made a decision there and then that the three remaining hot drinks, with their precious few calories, would all be Katelyn's and I didn't give a shit about the pains in my own belly.

It was around the same time the next day when I was standing by the final remnants of fuel, a towel and some picture frames that struggled to take to flame, that Katelyn came creeping towards me. I didn't notice her at first, she was so quiet and even with a blanket draped around her shoulders, I could see she was hunched over and tried to pin her shoulders against her ears in a pitiful attempt at keeping her neck warm.

"Hi, honey. Are you sure you're ok to be walking around?"

"Just had to go to the bathroom, but I don't feel as cold as I did." Sure enough, she'd stripped off to her New Forest Ladies jersey, which I wasn't sure was a great idea.

I felt her bare arm, which not to my surprise was like ice. "The second to last meal in this whole place." I held the mug up to her hand, which still clung to the cover.

She squinted. "But I thought the chocolate I had last night was my final meal. Are you sure you're counting correct?" Her eyes darted from side to side and perhaps it was wrong of me to use her jumbled state of mind to my advantage.

"Silly me, I must have counted wrong the other day. We still have another drink each after this one. I've just had mine, so this here is yours." I held it out for her and prayed my face didn't give it away.

Finally her face recognised that maybe, just maybe, I wasn't bullshitting her and, still clutching to the cover, she reached forward for the mug. Unfortunately, her hand blundered straight into it, sending the mug and its contents crashing to the floor. I saw it happen in slow motion and tried in vain to save the precious fluid.

But the most worrying thing of all was that her body didn't respond to the accident for a full one, maybe two seconds, an extremely late reaction to the clattering of a mug, as she made a pitifully small jump backwards, her jogging bottoms already soaked in hot fluid before she buried her face in her hands and began shaking her head. "I'm so clumsy." She tried stooping down toward the mess but her joints were so stiff that she grimaced in discomfort. She straightened and looked at me with defeated eyes. "I'm so sorry, Jess."

"Hey, that's ok. Don't you worry about that." I wrapped my arm around her shoulder and guided her back to bed.

I waited an hour before making the final sachet of hot

chocolate; any longer and the last of the fuel would have burned itself out. I still thought Katelyn might object to the chocolate so soon after spilling the last one, but the weight of that risk paled into insignificance.

This time I sat next to her in bed and held the cup to her lips. Her sips were small and I took her smile as a sign she enjoyed the beverage.

"What's the first thing you plan to do when you return to England?" I asked her, needing confirmation she remained hopeful more than anything else.

"A big Sunday roast and I don't care what day of the week it is."

I laughed, part in relief, part because Katelyn had earned the ability to make me laugh. "I wouldn't want to be the girl who stood between you and your Sunday roast. It sounds wonderful."

I tipped the mug to her lips, noting how their natural colour had drained. Indeed, her lips, ears and fingertips all had an alarming blue tinge to them.

"Well you should come too." She declared. "I make a pretty mean Sunday roast with all the trimmings."

I repositioned the covers, ensuring her neck was fully enclosed. "Why, thank you for the invitation, Katelyn. I'd be honoured to eat Sunday roast with you." And I really would too.

There was silence for a while before she spoke. "I'm so sorry I took James and for the pain I caused you."

"Oh, I forgive you for that. I'm over it." And as soon as I said it, I realised I *was* completely over it. In fact I hadn't thought about James once in the last couple of days, which really was a first since the breakup. Maybe it was because right now there were more important things on my mind or maybe, just maybe it was because I was falling in love with someone else.

She spoke again. "Sometimes I have to think hard about how I got here. But I know there was an avalanche. And I'm pretty certain something's happening to me." My heart sank and all I wanted to do was burst through the walls and take her to safety.

"Hey, don't you worry about anything. I'm going to take care of you." My voice cracked and for that I silently cursed.

She turned her head to me and as she did her lips pinched hard together, her eyes squinting. "You look just like that girl I had a crush on."

Then the fire burned itself out.

NO GAS, NO CLEAN WATER, NO ELECTRICITY, NO HEAT, no food.

But I would never give up because we still had each other.

In the three days since the fire burned out for the final time, we adapted the best we could.

I couldn't give Katelyn cold water as she lay in bed with hypothermia. But I evolved my methods to deal with the changing circumstances which, for the time being, had proven to be sufficient – Just.

I crushed the snow in the pan and watched it slowly turn to sludge. At first, I'd attempted using a dozen candles bunched together to heat the snow, but this proved worse than futile and besides, we were running low on candles. My next method was adequate if uncomfortable.

I poured the sludge into the plastic mustard bottle, closed the lid, lifted up the several layers of clothing that enveloped me and held the bottle against my belly. Thirty minutes later the liquid was acceptable for drinking.

I took another plastic bottle, filled with washing up liquid, and squirted the contents into a cup. Whenever I needed to pee, I did so in the bottle. It proved its worth immediately when I slipped into bed alongside Katelyn, wrapped my arms around her and crammed the warm bottle between our bodies.

We spent much time in this way as she shivered and I prayed my efforts would not be in vain. Her shivers transmitted to myself and I liked to think that we were exchanging bodily warmth; her cold to me, my warmth to her.

"Didn't we destroy them." Katelyn stuttered, referring to our last volleyball game, or so I assumed.

"We sure did. You played so well. 2016, you're off to Rio babe." I whispered gently into her ear.

"It's hot in Rio. That would have been nice."

"It *will* be nice. It *will* be."

The hunger had become easier to bear, to the extent that in comparison to the cold, we barely noticed it.

I had taken once again to wearing the nightclothes Katelyn lent me on our first night here together, for comfort as well as the extra warmth they provided.

Then, just like we always did, we drifted off in each other's arms.

I LAY WITH MY ARMS WRAPPED AROUND HER, OUR FEET tangled together, her head nestled on my shoulder, her snores punctuating the silence. The tiniest slit of light was shining in through one of the upper windows, no more than on the previous days, but it still gave hope that we weren't completely submerged in snow.

I'd had enough.

It was morning and I'd determined not to spend another day in this cabin. Nobody was coming to rescue us. If we were to live, then we, or at least *I* would have to do something about it.

I kissed Katelyn on the lips. Despite being chilled, the slightest hum came from somewhere inside her and for a second I thought I saw her lips move and the slightest hint of a dimple appear on her cheek, though I could have been wrong. I pulled away and wobbling slightly, stepped onto the floor.

I had to maintain contact with the wall as I stumbled in the direction of the fireplace. The hearth was covered in soot, but regardless, I lowered myself to my hands and knees and peered upwards. Through the narrow shaft, daylight, bright blue sky even, lay framed within the brickwork. The opening would not be large enough, not even for my head and not even if I used oil to grease my skin.

Shambling across the room, I opened the door and scowled into the wall of snow that may as well have been a wall of iron. Where we'd often created inlets into the snow as we foraged for clean water, I'd always been dismayed at how the snow from above would tumble into the opening like a never ending supply intent on keeping us trapped. Now, the wall stared back at me, unchanged, taunting and my eyes had become so accustomed to the gloom it almost hurt to stare at its whiteness.

"Hey." Katelyn croaked. "What are you doing?" She was sitting up against the headrest.

"I've had enough." I said as I approached her. "Today's the day we get out of here."

She shifted and looked hopeful. "You promise?"

I hesitated. I didn't want to break a promise, not to her. "I promise." I perched on the bed and wrapped my arms around her. Even now I could lose myself, intoxicated in her natural scent. And behind her I could see the window that mocked me from the above.

It was eight maybe nine feet off the ground and easily wide enough to fit through. I dragged the couch across and standing on the backrest I was able to press my face up to the glass. Again, I could see blue skies through the narrow gap in the top corner - Hope, perhaps.

My concerns were threefold. First, I didn't know if the glass would break, even though I knew I'd give it a bloody good go. Second, if I did manage to break it, then climbing out would be perilous. I envisioned myself tipping over the window and falling through the soft snow, enveloping myself and freezing to death and I wouldn't be much good to Katelyn then.

Finally, there was Katelyn. If I did manage to successfully smash through the glass and then make it out, there was no guarantee I'd be back with help and I'd be leaving Katelyn alone, in the cold made much worse by the fresh gaping wound in the shack. Still, the only alternative was death, that we'd both perish in the cold regardless and a chance at life was far better than certain death.

I searched for something I could use to smash through the glass and settled on the ironing board. It was metal, pointed at one end and long enough for me to stand at a safe distance from any smashed fragments.

Whilst Katelyn watched from our bed, I thrust the board at the window, though at first only with moderate intensity to determine what power would be required. It would require a lot more.

Again and again, I launched the board at the glass until a crack appeared. Encouraged, I concentrated on that area and

after a few more hits the crack spread to the rest of the window.
Despite the weakness that was overtaking my body, I managed
to summon enough strength and finally, the board plunged
through the glass.

I jumped back and the crash pierced my ears but that noise
was blunted by the aftermath and I was knocked off my feet as
the snow cascaded through the opening.

It rushed inside the cabin like an unstoppable force, the
roar of a waterfall crashing around my body. I tried to
scramble backwards but I'd landed badly and twisted my
ankle. The pain shot through my entire body, incapacitating
me and I had no choice other than to lay where I was as the
snow continued to flood inside and I knew it would only be
a matter of seconds until the snow began piling on top
of me.

Then a shadow was looming above and before I had chance
to turn my head, I was sliding backwards. Katelyn's arms were
linked around my waist as she pulled me slowly back. I don't
know how she had the strength and indeed, she found the
exertion almost debilitating, her grip quite feeble and for every
instant the snow continued gushing inside. But she continued to
pull me to safety.

I helped by adding my good leg to the struggle and we gained
enough purchase to reach safety and then I was heaved onto
the bed.

"Ouch." I cried as my foot struck the wooden frame.

And just as I began to worry we'd be engulfed by snow, it
stopped.

The giant pile of whiteness lay in a heap, almost like a slope
begging us to simply stroll up and leave the cabin. I doubted it
would be that simple, not just because I knew I'd sink into the

snow, but because, as I tried to remove my boot, my ankle was in agony.

"At least we have plenty of ice. You got the gin?" I tried to laugh, but it wasn't funny.

The blue sky shone into the cabin, flooding us with the first natural light we'd seen in days.

I WINCED AS I TRIED PRISING THE BOOT OFF MY FOOT AND wondered if my ankle had expanded. The leather felt like it was crushing me and I heaved one final time, gritting my teeth as Katelyn held my arm. But the shooting pain was too much and I collapsed in frustration and struck my fists repeatedly against the backboard. "Argh! I'm so sorry Katelyn, I just wanted to get us the fuck out of here." I felt the involuntary trickle of tears on my cheeks and lamented that she was seeing me like this.

"Hey, you tried and I'll always love you for that." She embraced me, made soothing sounds and then attempted to pull the blankets over us. Her hands fumbled with the doubled up covers, too cold to properly clasp them.

I sniffed and helped her with the blankets and then we laid there staring up at the ceiling, but not before I positioned her feet between my legs.

And then I exploded into laughter, a deep belly laugh that almost hurt and was completely inappropriate.

"What on earth could be so funny?"

"Oh, just everything." I thought about my opinion of Katelyn when I arrived in Italy. I had hated this girl more than anything. And all it took to change my feelings were an avalanche, a wrecked holiday, starvation, hypothermia and now a twisted ankle on top of everything else. "It's a wonder I haven't killed you yet."

I felt the distinct blunt shock in my side that could only come from being elbowed. Then Katelyn laughed and turned to face me. "There's still time. Nobody would ever know."

I turned to face her. "Oh, Katelyn that's just it. I couldn't kill you, not now, not after everything we've been through."

And then she closed her eyes. I held both her hands in mine and tried to pass on my heat. Occasionally, her fingers flinched and I wondered of what she was dreaming. I gazed into her beautiful features and I knew the truth but not why it had taken so long to realise it. The truth wasn't even buried deep down, trapped like a girl in an avalanche. Because when I looked at her and realised the person she'd made me, I wanted her to know the truth, what I knew in every fibre of my being.

"I love you." I whispered and I pressed my lips against hers.

I wanted Katelyn to know what she meant to me - And I would tell her.

I fell asleep.

ESSENCE

*T*he vibrations came first.

And I felt them mostly in my ears as the floor began shaking in an unfamiliar discord. Was I dreaming? Was my subconscious reliving the nightmare of the avalanche that would forever imprison us in this tomb.

I squeezed Katelyn tighter. If this was the end, then I would die with my arms around the one I loved. My only regret was that she would never know my true feelings, how she'd changed me as a person and altered the entire course of my life.

She opened her eyes and muttered wearily. "What...what's that shaking? My brain feels like its rattling in my head."

"I'm not too sure, it might be another avalanche." That nightmare thought came to me as I was saying the words and on cue my arms began shaking in unison with the floorboards. I panicked. "Katelyn, I really feel I need to tell you something... something that I realised these last few days and..."

My words were drowned out not by vibrations but by the

awful grinding and crunching that accompanied them. "What the hell is that?" Again, my voice was lost amidst the cacophony as Katelyn and I clung hard to each other.

A shadow slowly moved across the room and then there was temporary darkness as some giant machine rumbled past the window. A moment later light flooded through the second window and then the third as the snow disappeared - This was no avalanche. Could I dare to hope?

As soon as one intolerably loud din had faded another would begin and another, each time accompanied by darkness that temporarily enshrouded us - Machines, very big machines. Once that salvo too diminished, then another round began as if some giant force, or several giant forces were circling the cabin.

Our bed had moved several feet in the process, the vibrations had been that strong and being overwhelmed with joy, all kinds of other emotions and sensing we were out of time, I was just about to tell Katelyn those words when something happened.

It all happened in slow motion, the door flinging open and...

Two men, dressed in bright yellow coveralls strode inside. They spotted us immediately and ignoring the smashed up cabin and giant snow heap conspicuous against the wall, they rushed right over to us as we huddled in bed together.

"Signore, come state? Per quanto tempo siete stati qui?" The taller of the two asked as he scanned the interior with raised eyebrows and a gaping mouth.

"Troppo, molto troppo. Una settimana...piu? Siamo freddo e fame." I stared at Katelyn and felt my own mouth plunging. Just when you think you know a person.

We were helped to our feet and they half carried us toward the door. I took one final look at the cabin that was so nearly our tomb. In a way, I was sad to be leaving. This place had changed me. We'd survived but how would life be when things returned to 'normal?'

I passed through the cabin threshold as the beautiful mountain air hit me and, hobbling across the snow covered grass, my arm around my saviour, we made our way toward one of several waiting ambulances and I took a moment to gaze up at the blue sky, something I'd never take for granted again.

The source of all that noise turned out to be not one, not two, but three giant snow ploughs, house sized machines that were still working, pushing snow away from the other cabins. My attention then turned to three other large machines that sucked up the snow from one side of the vehicle before propelling it away at the other. I marvelled at the snow being flung into the forest in three continuous streams of white like it was nothing.

Too much, almost too late. Where were they days ago?

We were escorted inside and as the ambulance door closed behind us, as the sirens blared from above and we began to move, I knew my life was changed forever.

TO BE FAIR TO THE LOCAL MOUNTAIN RESCUE FORCE, WHO'D only discovered us thanks to a skier who'd spotted our cabin after the snow had been pulled inside by my smashing of the window, the rescue had been professional, once they knew we existed.

Amanda had made herself a local nuisance after being lucky enough to avoid the avalanche due to being with Marco, her Italian date at the time. She'd insisted repeatedly that her friends were buried alive in their cabins "somewhere near the town of Cortina," though because she could not remember the way, nor the name of where we were staying, 'Mortisa,' she had been dismissed as a crank by the local police force.

"I tried, I really did." She protested as she loomed over me in my hospital bed.

"Why didn't you just show them a map?" I asked, almost unable to comprehend how oblivious it was possible for some people to be at the age of twenty one.

In response she just gave a short shrug and that was that. Clearly she'd been spending way too much time with her Italian hunk and her teammates had been shoved way down the list.

"I won't be coming back to England, Jess. I like it here." She bounced once on her toes, the sexed up minx.

I thought better of asking her exactly what it was about Italian food, art, architecture and culture she liked so much. "Wow, so things with you two really took off?"

"I guess you can say that."

I was happy for her. Was it wrong that so soon after everything, my first thought was of taking her place on the team?

The doctors performed some tests, mainly using thermometers in different locations in and around my body to measure my core temperature. After deciding I was safely within acceptable ranges they gave me a warm sweetened glucose drink, much like the usual sports energy drinks, as a precaution. I wondered if the 'treatment' was more for the mild hypothermia or for the hunger. My ankle was checked over and luckily it turned out to be a mere bruise from clattering the ground so hard. I was lucky because it wasn't twisted, as I'd feared, not that it mattered given our ski time had been vanquished, and as for volleyball...

After remaining overnight in hospital, I still hadn't

consumed any solid food since the avalanche. By my reckoning, we'd been nine days buried beneath the snow and now ten days without food.

When we'd arrived at the hospital Katelyn and I had been rushed into separate rooms and I hadn't seen or heard from her since. The fact it drove me insane, not just the not knowing part, but the being away from her part, spoke volumes about my feelings for her. I prayed she was recovering, but I couldn't lay around in bed any longer waiting, I just had to know.

It took me fifteen minutes of wandering around the fourth floor of the hospital before I located her room. I peered in through the window to see her reclined in bed with a tube in her mouth - That bad? My heart struck against my ribcage and then she noticed me spying and beckoned me to enter. Relief.

She wasn't daft and being sensitive to the face I must have been pulling, was quick to ease my fears. "Hey, I know what you're thinking, so don't poop yourself, Jess." She gestured to the awful tube. "It's all just precaution."

The first thing I noticed upon entering was the warmth, the atmosphere being stuffy and quite uncomfortable. I picked up the chart at the end of the bed and it almost fell out of my grasp. "You have *mite ipotermia?*" I yelped it, whatever *it* was, in Italian it sounded bad.

She laughed. "You moose. It means *mild hypothermia.*"

The tension in my shoulders noticeably eased up, not just from hearing her prognosis, but from seeing how jovial she was about it. I replaced the chart and went to her side, noticing for the first time my sweaty palms. "Well you are sure full of surprises, miss." I also didn't like how high pitched my voice came out.

"How so?"

"About speaking Italian, you idiot." I teased her and she smiled. "I always knew there was something geeky about you."

"Oh, I'm really not that fluent. I have an Italian grandparent and have spent a few summers here in the past." She laughed and rubbed the back of her neck. "I'm ok though. I've always been quite susceptible to the cold, I just didn't know how much and I'd be a lot worse if it hadn't been for *you* taking care of me."

I flapped a hand feebly to dismiss it even though all I wanted was some physical manifestation of her gratitude. A prolonged hug and maybe a little smooch would have been awesome. That didn't happen though and instead I asked something banal yet important.

"What treatment are you getting?" I sat down beside her and held her hand, remembering too late my paws were leaking fluid. She gave me a squeeze and hope flooded through my entire body, my heart beat faster and I felt my cheeks turning red. That a person, a girl of all things, could have that kind of exhilarating effect on me from merely squeezing my hand said so much. But could I possibly dare hope there was something more behind it? What did it mean when a girl squeezed the hand of another girl? And why was I overthinking this shit so much?

"I guess this whole room is kind of my treatment." She began, her voice weary. "It's stifling in here. My core temperature was bordering on dangerous levels so they stuck me in this room and cranked up the heating. And this," she plucked at the tube, "this delivers a steady trickle of warm fluids straight to my gut."

"So how long are you in here for?" All I wanted to do was take Katelyn to the nearest restaurant with fast service and order everything on the menu.

"I'm not sure. But I feel fine...won't be too long. Have you eaten?"

"Babe, you have read my mind. I haven't. Not yet." I was contemplating adding that I was waiting for her before I ate anything but chickened out of saying it. My belly growled though, now we were discussing the subject. It had been quiet recently, perhaps because it had adjusted to the feeling of hunger. Though now something in my brain had been triggered and my mouth was also releasing an abundance of saliva.

"Well you really should." She insisted and my heart sank, which made me blurt out.

"I can't. It just wouldn't feel right eating while you're in here. I have to stay with you!" Oh, it sounded pathetic but I didn't care. It would take all of hell freezing over to pull me away from Katelyn after all we'd been through together.

Her face softened and she plucked again at that bloody tube. "The fluids I'm getting at least have protein in them. But they say I shouldn't eat until tomorrow because I have to be gradually weaned back on. But there's no way my first meal in God knows how long is going to be hospital food."

"I'll wait for you." And I would not take *no* for an answer, which is why I leaned over and kissed her on the cheek as I stood to leave, discussion over, and I was glad to see her accept it with a smile, though I could gauge nothing else positive from her reaction. Sometimes I hated not being a mind reader.

The next few hours I spent drifting the corridors searching for information. Unfortunately, I'd left my phone, along with all my belongings in the cabin and so I had to take any news as and when I could - And from whatever source.

I saw Marie first in the visitors' canteen.

"You're a bit fucking late aren't you?" She said through a mouthful of Panini with prosciutto. I required a few seconds to decipher it and then a few more to comprehend the meaning behind it, that I never arrived at her cabin.

"I think I have a pretty good excuse, my dear." I took the seat opposite and automatically began scrutinising her perceptible appearance for any obvious signs she'd been through an ordeal. She didn't notice.

"Yeah, if you say so. It's no wonder you lost your place on the team if *that's* how slow you are." She smiled as she said it, which made it ok. Only Marie could get away with dry remarks like that. "A full week all alone. Do you have any idea what that does to a girl like me? It nearly drove me insane."

"I can imagine. You seem fine though." I gave her another critical eye over. Where in my opinion, Katelyn and myself looked tired, gaunt and malnourished, Marie appeared lively and well fed, though of course, I wouldn't say *that* to her.

She exhaled and slammed a closed fist playfully against the table. "I like cake bars ok. And I couldn't risk not finding them over here so..." she trailed off and sucked in air, "...and I kind of, sort of, kind of, accidentally discovered the combination to Amanda's bag."

"Marie!" I laughed. "What did she have in there?"

She shook her head with incredulity. "Jess, that is one kinky bitch. I swear, I required many days to summon the courage to burrow further down amongst her twisted belongings. And that girl's supposed to be an athlete..." she tutted. "Oh, Jess, the amount of food she brought, you would not believe."

The talk of *food* again set my belly off. "Oh we really must change the subject."

"Jess, would you get something to eat, you look like you've lost a stone in weight." She stood and grabbed my arm but I pulled away and gave her an apologetic look.

"I'm sorry, I really can't. Not until Katelyn's ready."

She made a double take and needed a few seconds to respond. "Katelyn?...Katelyn?...Why do you care about that cow all of a sudden?"

I cringed inwardly. I hadn't really meant to mention her name and was struck by how hearing 'Katelyn' coming from the big mouth of Marie bothered me so much. "Um, well, I don't really, but you know, you can't spend days locked away with somebody and not become a little bit closer to them. It was either that or kill each other." I looked down at the table and muttered. "And she's not a cow."

"Uh huh, and when did you turn into such a lesbian?" She asked deadpan.

"Um, what?" I straightened. Why did she...

"...I'm joking, of course. But you should see your face." She sat back down and picked up her Panini. "But fine, I won't offer you any more food."

There was something I'd delayed asking her. "Marie, any news about everybody else?"

"You haven't heard?"

"Nope."

She held up a finger and I had to wait until she finished chewing. "From what I gather, it was you and your little lesbian lover who got the worst of it. Stewart had apparently packed a whole load of food and wine and he and Dorothy made a second honeymoon of it. From what I hear, Holly's in a bed in some hot room with a tube down her throat."

"Same as Katelyn." I said feebly.

She paused, squinted then continued. "Anyway, Amanda's trying to take credit for saving everyone but she soon quit that line when I managed to work out from her ramblings that for two days, she'd been blissfully unaware there'd even been an avalanche. Can you believe that? The sheer bloody minded stupidity. She'd shacked up with her Italian...I can't remember his name...the hot one. Moves fast does that one, not that I'm surprised after witnessing the contents of her luggage."

I shook my head. "So how did they, um, realise we were trapped?" I'd already heard two different versions and this was fast becoming like Chinese whispers.

"I don't know, but it seems fairly plausible to me that after day seven went by and a whole volleyball team never came home then people are gonna talk." She bit into her Panini, giving no thought to speaking with a mouthful. "I mean, weren't we supposed to play VC yesterday? I hope Burbridge enjoyed her visit to New Forest. Shit, we're gonna be docked three points for a *no show* now aren't we? There goes our chance of winning the league."

It was hard getting away from Marie and she tried but failed again to get me to eat something. She told me that the team had been accommodated, gratis, in a local hotel, but that we'd have to arrange our own flights home with the airline. I'd make an effort to politely forego the hotel myself to instead sleep on the chair next to Katelyn. After spending the last few nights cuddling up to her, a chair by her side was the best I could hope for.

As the elevator made its way up to the fourth floor, I looked forward to giving her the gossip, as well as the good news that, with only one real exception, everybody was ok.

I arrived outside Katelyn's door and was about to enter when I checked my step, distracted by the large figure I saw looming over her through the glass.

Something twisted in my belly, the figure was familiar to me, in fact I knew him very well.

James leaned down and kissed Katelyn hard and passionately on the lips, her fingers linking together around his back. The largest bunch of flowers I'd ever seen were crammed into a vase by the bedside.

I froze, intent only on torturing myself with the sight. I wanted to burst down the door and physically remove him. But was that what Katelyn would want? I'd only be making a fool of myself yet for her I'd do anything, but that? My skin turned white and I wondered if Katelyn would ever know my true feelings. She sure knew how James felt though, because at a moments notice he'd flown across Europe to show it, to be with his woman.

Still, I almost did burst through that door and make my presence known. But in the end, I chose to walk away, the image of them kissing burning a hole in my soul.

THE LOCAL PRESS WERE KEEN TO FILM US IN THE RESTAURANT of our hotel as we awaited the arrival of our breakfast. But Stewart and a couple of burly hotel security guards had succeeded in turfing them out onto the streets.

"Signore, they just want to know everybody is all right. Tourism is our lifeblood, we depend on the world knowing we're not complete incompetents here." The security officer reassured him.

"Well that may be, but some of these girls haven't eaten in a long time. So tell them to come back this afternoon." Stewart told him, knowing full well we'd be gone by then.

"Si, signore."

Finally, a waiter, with a seeming halo over his head, although I might have been imagining that, trundled in with a large trolley filled to the brim with several layers of breakfast goodies. After ten days I would carve that trolley a new arse and my mouth was salivating like a lion coming off hunger strike as my brain prepared my body for its first major intake of food in so long. My belly rumbled as my brain commanded blood to concentrate in that area to aid digestion. Oh, how the emotions made me feel fuzzy. Although Katelyn wasn't here, and I felt a pain in the chest because of it, the fact she was probably fine dining with her boyfriend kind of released me from the obligation to wait for her. I didn't feel guilty, about that at least, just extremely gutted.

The waiter was grinning as he approached but then his halo disappeared as some other diner intercepted him and began engaging him in conversation, the jerk, all while holding a half-eaten croissant, which he used to gesture toward his table because he required more jam.

"Oh my God, will you hurry up!" Marie shouted, startling half the diners in the room.

Then Stewart casually pulled out his chair, made his way towards the waiter, gently put his arm around his shoulder and then physically moved him in our direction, trolley and all. Sure it was maybe a little overly assertive, or borderline aggressive, but I think on this occasion I could look the other way.

"Scusate..." The red cheeked waiter, with a little help from Stewart, set the platters on the table one by one.

To see them though, so crammed full with Parma ham and melon and cheeses and breads and pastries and fruits and fish and meats and other stuff I couldn't even identify. And how we attacked those croissants and brioches and everything else with a relish never before seen in the Dolomite region.

It was sometime during round two of the exact same breakfast when Holly hobbled in with the aid of a stick. She took her seat and we all paused to give her hugs and a few of us began piling food onto her plate so she wouldn't have to wait a second longer.

"How'd you get here?" Dorothy asked.

"I checked out of the hospital with Katelyn and shared a taxi with her and her boyfriend."

"She's here?" I blurted out, almost startling myself.

"Yep, she's just in reception." Holly said, looking frail.

"That's so sweet of James, flying to Italy to make sure she's ok." Tina said from the other side of the table to various murmurs of agreement as I crushed the napkin in my hand.

Then they entered and there was no need for Katelyn to use a walking stick since James was only too happy to act as her support; her arm draped over his shoulder, his muscular arm around her midriff pulling her in close to him. I couldn't help but feel that should've been my job, if there was any justice, which clearly there wasn't.

James had brought her a change of clothes, for she wore a different pair of jeans that fitted her tightly and emphasised her thighs and the curves of her bum. It so wasn't fair, the injustice of the situation almost made me want to do some damage to him. She was also wearing her New Forest Ladies jersey above a shirt and sweater, hardly the height of fashion, but certainly functional considering her need to stay warm, but damn, she still looked so good and it killed me.

The girls nearest her, Marie excepted, stood and after hugs were exchanged, two of the girls shifted around the table to create a double space for them both. The questions were fired her way and she didn't seem daunted by all the attention because, let's face it, she was used to it. She mentioned me a few times in her responses and that was when we made eye contact for the first time since her arrival. As for James, he barely noticed my presence, so transfixed he was on Katelyn. Considering everything, that probably made it easier and a little less awkward.

His hand remained on her lap as she devoured her first meal in so long and I wondered what was going on in her head right now. It was all just another day in Katelyn world, back to normal, being the superstar and making my life a misery, only now it would be for reasons completely different to before, reasons I never thought could ever possibly happen. Did she feel anything for me? Or would I be discarded now she was alive and well and could have sex every day with her boyfriend?

And as she rubbed his lap in return, I could only ask myself whether I'd fallen for Katelyn too far, too fast and too hard.

IT WAS FUNNY IN A TRAGIC WAY. TWO WEEKS AGO I HATED Katelyn for being with James and now I hated James for being with Katelyn; well perhaps *hate* was too strong a word, though I still found the whole predicament ironic. But I was a young and healthy woman, discovering her true self and all thanks to my former nemesis, I'd come a long way over the last week. And I would always love her for that.

As we drove toward Venice in a brand new rented minibus to replace the one that had ended down the mountain on its roof, we weren't to know that Dorothy had a surprise in store for us.

Now, she stood and addressed us. The mood was a lot more subdued compared to the journey into Cortina d'Ampezzo so there was little need for her to shout for attention. "Girls, I know we've not exactly had the trip we all hoped for, but it would be a shame if we were to see none of this wonderful country. So since we have a few hours to spare before departing, we'll be taking a slight detour to Verona." She must have seen the various looks of puzzlement on our faces because a few seconds later she threw up her arms and rolled her eyes. "Honestly girls, I give up sometimes. Verona as in *Romeo and Juliet*."

I really should have known that one. Perhaps recent events had damaged my brain functioning.

Twenty minutes later, the bus was pulling into Verona and with no snow in sight, what could go wrong?

Verona turned out to be like nothing I'd ever seen. In order to enter the old city, we had to walk under the Porta Borsari, a triple tiered Roman gate which, despite its two thousand year age, was still perfectly intact. From there our group walked down a narrow yet busy street lined with fashionable shops and I could easily picture the locals from two thousand years before trading and chatting and drinking, it was that kind of place with that kind of feel. The place oozed history which really made me realise my entire existence on this planet was a mere blink of an eye. All the more reason to make the most of it while I was alive, after all, things were almost very different.

"Oh my God! Did you see that Valentino handbag?" Marie shrieked from my flank, obliterating my philosophical train of thought.

The main square, Piazza Bra, was where stood the most stunning amphitheatre I'd ever seen. It completely dominated the square around which, dozens of restaurants and cafes were sited. We each did the usual tourist thing and had our photos taken on our phones. And then Stewart beckoned for us all to join together into two ranks so that he could take a group shot. I stood on the outside of the back row, one out from Dorothy. James stepped out from the photo, realising he wasn't a female volleyball player, but then Katelyn, who was crouching at front and centre called for him to return. He didn't protest and rushed back over to where they both crouched with their arms around each other before Stewart took the photo. I hoped I wasn't snapped scowling in their direction because that would be pretty hard to explain.

As we continued strolling around the city I hung back and linked arms with Marie.

"You're being very quiet today." She paused and seemed hesitant to say whatever was on her mind, which was odd for her. "Don't think I've not noticed who you've been gawping at."

"Excuse me?" I squealed. Had she been spying on me? "I have not been *gawping* at anybody... Who?"

"You know damn well who. The girl you absolutely hated the last time I spoke with you. You were willing to do anything to get away from her and now you're staring at her with puppy dog eyes." She pulled me closer in a gesture of comfort.

But this wasn't good. I'd already experienced being the object of everybody's gossip, which hadn't made my misery at the time any easier, but if things had been inconvenient after my breakup with James then I could probably expect the scandal to be ten times worse if word got out I was now lovestruck for the girl who'd taken him from me. Just thinking about that ridiculous scenario made me want to quit the team right now, whilst endeavouring to spend my few remaining months at

Southampton avoiding everyone I knew - And Marie of all people. Nope, this needed squashing at once.

"Marie, I have no idea what you're talking about, I really don't. So, if you wouldn't mind not thinking about this any further it would be appreciated. I mean, come on. The very notion is just insane. Just say it to yourself and see how it sounds. No, on second thoughts, please don't." And then I realised that even as I protested I was busy staring a hole in Katelyn's backside, even as she walked in front of us, holding hands with James. Oh, I was in deep fucking shit.

But the drama queen wasn't having any of it and even though I assumed she was probably joking, it didn't help. "Ok, so whatever...look...I don't care. So you made friends while you were holed up in your little love nest. I can understand that. But if I find out that anything else happened and you chose not to tell me, then Jess, you'll be bloody thankful there's no place on the team for you anymore because mark my words, if you keep me from my gossip then I will hunt you down!" And I believed it.

But I'd give her credit for one thing – She had the uncanny ability of striking me dumb. "I...I, Marie...I..."

She shook her evil head and cackled. "Yeah, I think your overall demeanour says so much more than your failed words ever could."

I gathered my composure as quickly as a girl who'd narrowly escaped death could. "Marie, what makes you think there's anything going on with Katelyn and me? In case you haven't noticed," and I jabbed a finger in the direction of Katelyn and James, "she has a bloody boyfriend. Look! See?"

Marie laughed and pulled me into her side again. "Between

you and I, I reckon James is about as frustrated as you are right now."

I straightened and almost hit this annoying person. "And what does that mean?"

"It means, Jess, that even though I'm getting the vibe of a girl who's gagging for it coming from you, I'm getting a similar vibe coming from *him*." And she nodded at the tall, broad man to my fore, with his wavy blond hair and masculine walking style. The two of them were only seven or eight metres in front and I prayed the volume from Marie's big mouth wouldn't carry on the breeze.

Though even I had to admit, she'd more than piqued my interest with this latest line of gossip, the subject was Katelyn after all, and that James was also 'gagging for it.'

I tried to sound nonchalant. "Oh no, Marie, I'm sure James is thoroughly satisfied right about now, can't you tell?" It pained me to say it, but it was the only thing I could think to say that would prompt her to spill what she knew, without incriminating myself further in this lesbian love triangle she already suspected.

She cocked a sceptical eyebrow. "Oh, you really are stupid. Well, that's what you get for paying too much attention to your studies and not enough on your teammates."

I exhaled in frustration. "Marie, what are you talking about? What do you know about Katelyn?" I demanded, almost losing all self-control.

She turned on me suddenly with bright eyes. "Hah! I knew it. You are such a slut." She was good. She was very, very good. And I was so far out of my depth.

"Marie?"

"Oh no. No, no, no, no, no slut. I can see I've pushed your

sexual buttons here, so if you want any more out of me, then I'm afraid you're gonna have to spill."

I flushed red and yelped out. "Marie, I have nothing to spill." How had she done this to me? I felt as though I was about to burst. What precious information was she withholding?

"I want to know exactly what went down in that sordid little love hole of yours." She said, batting aside my claim to innocence.

I was fully vibrating by this point, my mouth almost salivating like it was breakfast again. And she was doing it deliberately, knowing full well what keeping hold of this info was doing to me. And the little minx was loving every second of it. But I just couldn't. I'd only just admitted my feelings for Katelyn to myself and I was still far from coming to terms with all the implications that entailed. It would kill me, but I would not engage in gossip with this girl, Marie of all people, no matter what she thought she knew about Katelyn and me.

"I'm sorry, Marie, but all that went down in that cabin was a lot of sleep in order to preserve energy."

And now I had the pleasure of watching her face clam up in frustration. She squeezed my arm.

"Ouch, that hurt!"

"Yeah, whatever. Don't think I'm not keeping my eye on you." And I knew she meant it.

And then ironically, or what I thought at the time to be the universe playing a cruel trick on me, the group arrived at 23 Via Cappello, Casa di Giulietta.

We weren't the only tourists around by far, but we were the most conspicuous; a team of female volleyball players tends to draw eyes. Katelyn in particular caused a small stir when, in the heat, she removed a few layers of clothing to pose beside the statue of Juliet - I guess she was feeling better now. A small group of Japanese tourists, both male and female around our age, found the girl extraordinary as they made small bows and took their own photos of her. I was curious about what it was they found so interesting and came up with two possibilities. Either she looked like some major Japanese celebrity, which I found unlikely, or they were making a big deal over her breasts, which I found a near certainty. James meanwhile was lapping up the attention being given to his girl, as he leaned against the wall with Katelyn's discarded sweater flopped over his arm, a rather annoying grin plastered across his face.

Then James sauntered over and pulled her below the famous Juliet balcony as he handed his camera phone to Stewart to take the snap, but not before he planted his lips on hers; ugh, one of *those* photos. It was all just a little too much to take and so I turned away desperately needing to avert my eyes, only to find someone else stood very close.

"You are just obsessed with her!" Marie, of all people, and I wondered how close and for how long she'd been there, evidently taking notes. The girl was more obsessed than I was.

But it was all too much in the moment as the heat surged through me and I pushed past and began striding in the direction of Via Cappello and its wide open space, away from Marie and Katelyn and James and people. When I arrived back in the street I fanned my face and breathed as the cobbled road seemed to spin.

I was in deep shit!

What was happening to me? I'd never experienced anything like this before; not for James, not for anything or anyone. I'd never considered myself a lesbian. Sure I could look at other girls and appreciate their beauty, but as far as I knew, most girls did that kind of thing and besides, I'd always liked men, or so I thought. But now, looking at Katelyn, especially after leaving the confines of our cabin, scared me to my very core. I wanted nothing more other than to explore these feelings and I needed to explore them with *her*. The problem was James, my ex, just a minor complication there.

"Hey, I'm sorry, perhaps I shouldn't be so in your face all the time." Marie had followed me out into the street. "I can see now how this is really getting to you."

I exhaled and wiped my eyes. "Maybe it's just a phase, Marie. This isn't like me at all." I realised then I'd just admitted my feelings for Katelyn to Marie, without actually saying it, which also meant I'd said it out loud to myself too. If I were to ask Marie then she'd tell me what she knew about Katelyn, but I couldn't bring myself to do it. What if it wasn't what I needed to hear? She was, after all, acting out the part of *girlfriend*, with her boyfriend.

Marie gave me a squeeze. "Hang in there. It'll all work itself out."

"I just don't know what to do about it."

I'd spent too much time over recent months wallowing in self-pity over a guy. Now, I was due an even greater amount of pain, this time for a girl. Oh how I desired nothing more than to return to our little prison, just the two of us; the hunger, the cold, boredom, uncertainty, fear; just her and I.

How I never knew being 'rescued' would be the beginning of my troubles.

HOME

I was still unsure of what I was going to do. The volleyball league decided to reschedule our game against Worthing VC for nine days hence, enough time for us to recover from our ordeal and put in a few training sessions. Whether or not I'd be there was what I had yet to decide.

It wasn't only that during my darker moments I pictured Katelyn and James together that really bothered me. It was more that throughout the two days since returning to England I'd not heard a single thing from her. Not a phone call, text message or anything else. Though considering we'd said nothing to each other since the hospital, perhaps it wasn't surprising.

Had she forgotten about me? Did I not mean anything to her? Or had other 'distractions' taken her mind off all else. Evidently the status quo had returned, of one not existing to the other, and of my anguish.

I frequently found myself fantasising about that night by the open fire, applying a wet cloth to Katelyn's clear, smooth, beautiful skin, taking extra care with her breasts. We then kissed and it was like being in heaven as our souls connected. It had actually happened, I remembered it so vividly and so I knew I wasn't going insane – Or was I? It took a willpower I didn't know I possessed to stop myself from climaxing over those memories. I just couldn't do it. The pain. I couldn't bear to touch myself whilst thinking only of her. But another part of me knew I was holding out for that perfect time when maybe, just possibly, I'd be sharing a bed with Katelyn once more.

Everything else paled into insignificance by comparison, the awkwardness around work and home. I had no shifts scheduled at Starbucks for a few more days and if Chris felt embarrassed around me, then if he showed it, I didn't notice. For the most part I occupied myself by studying as hard as I always did, even if spending long periods trying to concentrate proved a challenge.

I found that taking frequent breaks and occupying myself with mundane chores helped to distract my mind. And so it was during lunch time of the third day when I was at the supermarket trying to decide which rice to buy when I felt my phone vibrate in my pocket. I pulled it out and it was then that my heart skipped a beat. The screen displayed the name - Katelyn.

I don't know why I checked over both shoulders, as if to make sure nobody could see my thoughts, though I enjoyed two or three deep breaths as I savoured the moment. What did she want?

I pressed 'read' and stared wide eyed at Katelyn's message. 'Hey, guess you no longer want to talk now you don't have to x.'

And then it occurred to me.

Not only had she been avoiding me, but I'd also been

avoiding her. All it had ever required was one person to initiate contact and days of moping about the house in a state of depression could have been avoided. So she had initiated contact with me – But could I read anything into it? While I wanted to believe that she missed me and lay thinking about me, for the good of self-preservation, my brain told me to play it cool.

I sent her a response. 'Hey, sorry, of course I'd like to talk to you. How about a drink tonight?' I hit send. Shit – That was in no way playing it cool and I instantly regretted my neediness.

Within seconds the reply came back. 'It's on! Meet at 7 pm in Oasis.'

My heart soared. It was one of those defining, memorable moments that come about only a few times in a person's life. Where I'd remember exactly the clothes I was wearing, the spot I was standing and even that the supermarket was playing One Direction over the speakers. Damn I hated One Direction, but that song would forever remind me of this moment. I yelped out in sheer joy, not giving a damn about anyone else on the aisle who might be judging me. Everything was a blur anyway.

But I had so much to do. It was half twelve in the afternoon and I took the bus straight over to my friend Debbie who ran her own mobile hairdresser and beautician business. Sure, she could have come to me, but that would have wasted valuable seconds. I had a facial and then she set to work on my hair, giving me a cut and blow dry. Then I returned to Southampton city centre and picked up a dress I'd had my eye on for a while; a beautiful black halter neck design that emphasised my figure whilst remaining classy and sophisticated, even if I did say so myself.

When I returned home I still had three hours to spare, which I knew would tick by painfully slow. As I tried running down the clock by keeping myself busy, I couldn't help but wonder if I was making too much of an effort. What if Katelyn just decided to throw on any old rags and turn up late looking dishevelled? No matter – She'd still look stunning regardless. But damn it, I hoped I wasn't setting myself up for a gigantic fall.

AT PRECISELY 6:55 PM I ARRIVED AT OASIS AND TOOK A SEAT at the bar.

I looked awesome! I'd made damn well sure of that and although I was the only person in the bar at this early hour, I'd still turned the heads of the doormen as I entered. My black dress was everything I'd hoped it to be and my heels emphasised my legs. I'd worn my hair down and my blonde locks contrasted beautifully against the colour of my dress.

I was on a date with Katelyn – I kept saying to myself, ignoring my previous good counsel not to get my hopes up too much, but I just couldn't help it. No matter what happened tonight, the truth was that even though I'd find it excruciatingly difficult, I'd still settle for being her friend rather than nothing at all. Regardless, I still hoped that she also thought of tonight as a *date*.

6:57 pm – My hands were clamming up and I caught myself looking again and again at the door.

6:58 pm – Checking my phone. No text messages telling me she'd be late – We were still on.

6:59 pm – She entered!

And *that* I was not expecting...

...In fact it took me a while to put my finger on it, as Katelyn strode toward me, but there was something different about her.

Sure, she was wearing light blue jeans which were a little too baggy to what I'd become accustomed to seeing her in. Sure, she donned a sleeveless white t-shirt with a picture of some band I'd never heard of on the front. But there was something else too, and it bothered me not knowing what it was. Then it occurred to me that this was only the second time I'd seen Katelyn outside of a volleyball team setting. Was this how she always dressed? – Like a lesbian?

"Hey, come here you." She opened out her arms and almost squeezed the air from my lungs. Lavender hit me immediately, bringing back memories of our cabin. "You look confused, Jess. Did the barman ask for your number or something?"

I hit her on the arm, her t-shirt definitely brought out the slight bulge of her biceps and I thought back to the awesome power she displayed during our last volleyball game; it was obvious where it came from.

The seconds past and I realised I still hadn't managed to utter a single word to my crush.

"You look fantastic, by the way." Katelyn said, her hand still touching my midriff.

"Um, yes, you look fantastic too." My words sounded inadequate, even to my own ears.

She grinned, as though being out of my depth in this situation was cute to her. "Let me buy you a drink." She beckoned over the barman. "I'll have a vodka and cranberry and..." she looked to me.

"And I'll also have a vodka and cranberry."

She grinned again and as she turned back to the barman, all I could do was roll my eyes at my own social awkwardness.

The drinks were placed down, Katelyn grabbed them and nodded toward the far corner of the bar. "Let's find a seat."

Finding a seat would not be a problem. The only other people in the entire bar were two middle-aged men having some kind of a business meeting. A group of isolated booths were set into the wall and I slid along the bench of the middle booth and positioned myself close to the wall. Katelyn slid along the bench opposite and with the tables being so large, it felt like there was a Russian steppe between us.

My foot immediately began tapping the floor. "So, um, how's your day been?" Straight away – Feeble. Where was all that old disrespect and animosity that used to get me through being so close to this girl? She'll see straight through you, Jess.

If she noticed my stiffness, she showed no sign. "Busy. I feel the need to jump straight back into everything. There's no way I'm taking things easy, they can go shove themselves." I assumed 'they' referred to the doctor. "I've been in the gym every day, eating as much chicken and fish as I can stuff inside my belly and trying to fit in some study whenever I can. How about you?" God, she really was so beautiful, it almost hurt. Her hair was in its usual style of left alone to roam and with every movement of her head large flocks of the stuff bounced off her shoulders. The spotlight from above shined over her, giving her brown locks a special kind of glow and all I wanted to do was bury my nose in it. She sipped from her straw and I seized the opportunity to glance downwards to where her breasts were stretching out her t-shirt, the band's name was The Wild Life. Hmm, I'd have to give them a look.

By the time she replaced her drink I was making eye contact again. "I've been knuckling down with study, but I don't start back at work for a few days. I'm thinking of joining the gym, but it's dependent upon my decision with regards to the team."

"What? Are you still thinking of quitting? Even now? Jess, I know you don't hate me anymore, at least not like you used to." She said the last part with a smile and displayed her perfect teeth.

What with being buried beneath an avalanche, making a decision on my volleyball future had taken a back seat recently. When I thought about things right now, if it hadn't been for New Forest Ladies, I'd never have met Katelyn.

"Well I guess I don't *hate* you anymore, Katelyn..." her hands were resting face down on the table and all I wanted to do was reach across to hold them. Damn but the table was huge and even if I had the bottle, which I didn't, there'd be no way my arms would stretch that far without it coming across as being forced. Instead I had to settle for eye contact and now I noticed that in comparison to most other occasions we'd been together, she wore very little makeup, not that she needed it anyway. "... No, how could I hate you after everything? I really don't know. Yes, I should probably fight for my place, but I'd only be fighting against you." And yes, I realised how that sounded.

I didn't know it, but my own hands were on the table in a gesture mirroring hers. Her hands slid forward a few inches, before they changed their minds and retracted.

"Jess, that's so sweet."

"I mean, I didn't mean it like..." but I very much did.

She pressed her lips together. "It'd be such a shame. You're so talented and I swear you have eyes in the back of your head. And you're quick. Plus we'd never get to hang out."

Whoa, my heart skipped another beat there. "Katelyn..."

"...I mean, you and I with the team. We'd all miss those days."

Back down to earth.

I exhaled. "They really were some of the best days of my life.

Well, give or take being substituted and replaced by a genetic freak."

She laughed, which thankfully eased some of the tension and then she sipped her drink, prompting me to do the same. But as we placed our glasses down, there was still an uneasiness that remained, at least which I felt. She on the other hand appeared content with the silence and to study my discomfort. It wasn't bad necessarily. There's a fine line between nerves and that wonderful feeling of butterflies. I had both right now, which had to count for something. There was so much I needed to discuss with her but the difficulty was broaching the subjects in the first place. Marie popped into my head, a girl I really didn't want to be thinking about right now, but God damn, she certainly wouldn't beat around the bush and waste any time. Nope, Marie would simply yell out to Katelyn, "I want you!" And that would be that. Damn her.

"You're in deep thought about something, Jess." How did this girl always manage to read me so well? It was like Katelyn could see into my soul. Either that or I was just plain easy to read. "What are you thinking about?"

"Oh, nothing." And why did I always struggle so much to be frank and open with Katelyn? Was I really so afraid of the unknown?

"I know what it is, Jess."

"You do?" I asked with too much enthusiasm.

She laughed. "Right there...see! There's obviously something."

"Stop teasing me, Katelyn."

She smiled from the mouth, not from the eyes. "Jess, I tried to tell you back in our cabin...I've been there."

"You've been where?"

"Where I'm pretty sure you are right now. And it really wasn't all that long ago and I probably still would be there if it weren't for..." she trailed off.

How could she have any clue what I was going through? But at least the subject had finally been raised, kind of. "You know where I am now? And *what* really wasn't all that long ago?"

She exhaled and closed her eyes as her hands once again attempted to make their way over to mine and this time I very nearly reached out myself. "You remember my *friend* Grace?"

"Grace? No." Unless it was... "...you mean the girl you brought to our end of season ball last year?" I vaguely remembered her, a striking redhead with a killer body. And if this Grace girl was who I was beginning to think she was then right now, I was even more envious of her than I was of James.

"Yes! The tall redhead..." she saw my facial expression and went down a different path, "...well, she was...we were kind of in a relationship."

I hated hearing it, but it was a long time ago and a lot had happened since then. It was now or never. "So, Katelyn...you are interested in women?" My entire arm was shaking as I clutched hard to my glass. "I mean, you stole my boyfriend!"

She wasn't expecting that because she flinched and leaned back. "Ok, Jess. I'm going to tell you everything. You deserve to know the truth." She had my full attention. Nothing else in the world existed right now. "I was where I think you are right now. I was confused, not quite sure about things inside my own head. Grace was already out in the open and although I was pretty sure I loved women, I wasn't ready to announce it to the world. I loved her company, she was exciting and so much fun, but there was just no let up with the pressure to try new things." She shook her head and looked briefly regretful. "For a while she had been pressuring me into meeting some of her, um, friends..." she saw my alarm and quickly moved to reassure me by holding up a placating hand, "don't worry, I never did anything with them, I'm not *that* kind of a girl, Jess. No, no, no, I'm monogamous. Once I'm in a relationship then that's it. But after she'd introduced me to some of her people, apparently she'd been pestered about it ever since, about trying some pretty wild things, stuff I'm not into, from both women *and* men." She shook her head and rolled her eyes. "That's the kind of girl she was and good luck to her, but it's not me. There was more to it, mostly that we were both very different people and things kind of came to a head that night at the ball when she ran out on me and that was that. I've not heard from her since other than a few angry text messages and could I please return her crap, blah, blah, blah."

So, Katelyn *did* like women and although I felt uncomfortable with the thought of another girl being that close to her, she'd done nothing wrong, according to her story, at least where Grace was concerned. And it was a relief to know she'd not been putting herself about like her ex obviously had. Of course, that wasn't yet the whole story.

She hesitated before continuing. "Jess, once again, I'm *so* sorry about James. I wasn't in a good state that night and I saw how happy you were and I wanted to take that from you. It truly was the worst thing I've ever done in my entire life and I did it to the one person who deserved it the least."

I squinted and shuffled in my seat. "But you already knew you liked girls?"

She nodded. "Fucked up, ain't it. But that's how I was and at the time I didn't care. I just wish I could change things."

This was all well and good, receiving an explanation and an apology, but there was still one thing. "You and James are still dating." I sounded savage and again, she was quick to reassure me.

"Jess, it's over between us. I ended it the day we arrived back in England."

What? Really? Now, *that* was a revelation and my heart soared. "And what made you end it?" I knew what I hoped the answer to be, but I definitely needed to hear it.

She opened out her palms. "Oh, Jess, it was all a sham. But if one good thing did come of it then it was that it helped me see the truth, that he wasn't for me. That *it* wasn't for me."

"And what helped you decide that? Did you not enjoy him fucking you?" I could hardly believe my own words, but I'd found it too hard to use a different term to describe the act. Katelyn and James *lovemaking* was the last thing I wanted to hear myself say, even if I would still torture myself with the question.

She came straight out with the answer. "Jess, I want you to believe me when I say...nothing like that *ever* happened."

I landed back in my seat with a thump. Was I really supposed to believe that? "Oh come on, Katelyn. What do you take me for?" I'd always assumed they were fucking, it was logical, but it didn't lessen my love for her regardless. What was important now was that everything was out in the open, the truth, whatever that truth may be.

"It's true!" She insisted. "I know how it must sound and there's no way I can prove it to you, but it's the truth." And there was something there, in her tone and manner that made it believable. I wanted her, I knew that, and if we were to begin something here, then I had to trust her when she was adamant nothing sexual had ever happened between them. And the important thing for me was that it was no longer the thought of her being with James that mattered, but that she liked women; that she knew it and I knew it.

I looked her in the eyes and reached forward with my hands, hers came to meet mine and instead I grabbed ahold of her wrists. "Katelyn, did you and James ever have sex?" Again, the point wasn't whether or not they had, I just needed to know I could trust her.

She never looked away and spoke with conviction. "No. Not even once." She smiled and made a playful expression. "Not that he didn't try."

All I could do was laugh at that, the ego was back. "Oh, I can relate to it." Because I remembered so well myself, the pressure James had put me under to give it away. Poor James. Looks like Marie had been right, that he truly was frustrated.

My heart soared and I closed my eyes to savour the wonderful feeling of the butterflies and the heavy pounding of my heart and the lightheadedness and something else that words could never hope to describe. It was all just too good to be true.

Katelyn tilted her head. "And you can't hide these things from me, I *know* we feel the same about each other."

Time stopped. Nothing else existed other than Katelyn and me, right here and right now. I had the overwhelming need to touch her, to kiss her, to hold and caress her.

She must have read my mind because at once she stood, slid out from the bench and came around to my side, sliding along next to me so that her thigh pressed up against my own, quite a thrill. I turned to meet her eyes, her pupils dilated. "Jess, I never thanked you for saving my life."

I flapped a feeble hand, um, accidentally brushing her arm as I did. "Oh, Katelyn, I never did anything that..." she touched a finger to my lips.

"...You saved my life." She insisted and removed her finger and then she was leaning into me, slowly, her eyes closed. My God this was really happening. Lavender filled my world and then...

"...Evening ladies. How are ya both tonight?"

It was two big lads, hulking in their t-shirts as they moved into the empty space across from us. The slightly more muscular one with tattoos of eagles and daggers down both arms sat closest to the aisle and slammed down four glasses of beer. "Here ya go girls, enjoy yourselves."

Talk about annihilating the moment. "Um, thanks." I said, scowling at the pair of them as my nails dug into my leg.

The tattoo gestured to his buddy. "This is Paul and I'm Gareth." And then they held out their hands which we took out of politeness.

"Hello. I'm Jess, this is Katelyn."

Their hands were large and rough and they lingered for a time that was bordering on becoming creepy.

"Girls, you're both very beautiful. We spotted ya the moment we came in and had to come over and get to know ya." Paul declared, forgetting the only competition for our attention were a couple of middle-aged businessmen. "How's your evening been?"

Katelyn straightened and cleared her throat. "Look guys, it's really nice of you and we appreciate it, but we were just about to head off. We both have classes early tomorrow and we need to get some study in. But thanks." Katelyn made to leave and grabbed my hand beneath the table, another thrill, despite the company.

Gareth was quick to react. "Whoa, not so fast, love. We just bought ya both a drink. You at least owe us a few minutes of ya time." And then he put his meat hook on Katelyn's shoulder and pushed her back down into her seat.

I did not like that one bit. Nobody puts their hands on my girl and I'd have stood and slapped the creep, if only I wasn't wedged so tightly in by the wall. Instead I had to settle for verbally reprimanding him. "How dare you put your filthy hands on her!"

Paul reached over and touched my hand. "Whoa, settle down, love, he didn't mean anything by it. Let's just start again, shall we?"

I yanked my arm away. "Start again? He doesn't deserve it after that."

Katelyn turned into me and spoke soothingly. "Hey, Jess, it's ok." Then she stood and I stood with her. "But we *are* leaving."

Gareth snorted and a vein popped out of his neck. "Good fucking riddance. See Paul, I told you the brawny one was a fucking dyke."

It's happened only a few times in my life, when a red cloud falls over my vision and I temporarily lose all control and before I even knew what was happening I was reaching for the beer they'd so kindly purchased and before I could stop myself the contents were hurtling towards his bald pate. It was a perfect shot, even if I do say so myself, and within a second the golden liquid was soaking his face, t-shirt and tattoos.

We were quick and left, hand in hand, while they were still too stunned to react, exiting the bar with all kinds of chemicals and adrenaline flooding my system, only slowing to a walk after reaching the quay.

"That was close, but bloody fun." I panted into her ear, taking in a dose of lavender. "Where now?"

She had the answer and I wouldn't argue. "I live on Portland

Terrace, about ten minutes away. You're coming back with me and I'm not taking *no* for an answer." She grinned in a devilish way I'd not seen before, but my God, was it ever thrilling.

Something made me turn around, caution, instinct maybe and it was a good thing I did. They were coming after us.

"Um, Katelyn…" I tugged at her hand and jabbed a finger down the quay, from where they were trying to run, weighed down by their bulk, tattoos and half inebriated with drink. "We'd better be quick."

Her grip on my hand tightened and we ran along the quay in the direction of the city centre. Katelyn was a fast runner and usually I was too, but while she was wearing jeans and trainers, I was in heels and a black dress. They were gaining ground to such an extent that in under a minute we could hear their feet slapping at the concrete painfully close behind. At this rate they'd soon catch us and who could know what two angry men, who'd been embarrassed by two girls, would do then.

We panted hard, but I hoped they'd be panting harder and then we arrived in a more populated area with open shops, restaurants and bars; plenty of places to get lost in. We found a H&M clothes store, strolled through to the back, taking a few items of clothing along the way and entered one of the changing cubicles. I closed the curtain behind us and was then physically turned around by Katelyn. She was glistening from the exertion and possessed a look that told me more than words ever could. I knew I had the same expression plastered over my face – I want to fuck you now!

"We should probably stay here a few minutes, just until they give up the chase." Katelyn groaned into my ear as she pressed her thighs into mine.

I could gladly remain here with Katelyn all evening, but I

wanted just as bad to have her naked on her bed. I was conflicted, all right. "I'm sure we can occupy our time in..."

She didn't wait and I didn't need asking. Her hands were suddenly and forcefully on my hips and then I was pinned against the wall, the thud doubtless loud enough to startle whoever was in the next cubicle. Her hands were then in my hair as she moved her face up to mine, our lips an inch apart as she crushed her hips against me. My hands were seizing both her breasts through her t-shirt and she let out a high-pitched sigh. She breathed fast and heavy, the slight tang of cranberry on her breath.

My God, but would she please just kiss me, I'd waited so long it was almost unbearable. She must have read my mind because then her lips were against mine, pressing hard as our tongues connected and experienced the other. I shivered as her hand moved down my back and she clutched my ass and pulled me harder into her, our thighs rubbing together. It was raw passion of the like I'd never experienced and there were no words for the excitement that was building to a crescendo. I would explode if I could not have her in bed soon.

I pulled my lips away from hers but kept my hands on her breasts. "We have to go. They'll be gone now, surely...I'll take my chances. How far to your house?"

"Not long...a few minutes." She heaved. "Damn, Jess, but I need you." Oh, the look she gave me, and it was obvious this could quite easily escalate if we didn't leave soon.

It might have been a good idea to leave separately, just for the usual decorum purposes, but that thought left my head as soon as it appeared. I didn't give a shit who saw me walking out of the store holding Katelyn's hand, but more to the point, there was no way I'd risk being separated from her, even for a second.

We pushed aside the curtain and strolled out, our hair looking all kinds of messed up and passed a small crowd of gawpers queueing for the changing cubicles. I grabbed her hand, my face flushing from Katelyn, not from their stares and we made our way toward the exit, a distinct slickness between my legs reminding me this was really happening. There was no sign of our tattooed friends, not that they were at the forefront of my considerations right now.

It wasn't late, maybe a little past eight in the evening but the streets were still active with shoppers and people out for a fun time. Blending into the crowd was easy but the walk still took longer than I'd hoped.

"Not far now, Jess." She squeezed my hand in excitement as we finally turned on to Portland Terrace. "Just so you're aware, I have housemates. They're probably not in, but in case they are, one of them kind of has a crush on me."

"Hah, well I can kind of understand that."

We entered the mid-terrace Victorian flat which to me looked like the typical student accommodation with dishes piled in the sink, rubbish overflowing from untied plastic bags strewn by the door, junk and clutter almost everywhere and a traffic cone or two in the hallway. But it was the strange bouncing noise emanating from down the corridor that made me stop.

"What the heck is that?" I asked.

"Oh, you're about to find out."

Then, a large curly haired student, on a space hopper no less, came bouncing around the corner grasping a Bud in one hand. "Kaaaatelyyynnn! Come join me on here."

I couldn't help but smile at the strange spectacle. For one, the ball looked like it would explode at any minute as he compressed the thing almost as far as physics would permit. I'd have to humour this, as frustrating as it was in the moment.

"Nice try, but not this time."

"Can't blame a lad for trying." He gestured to me with his beer. "And who is this?"

I waved at him. "Hi, I'm Jessica."

"Nice to meet you Jessica, I'm Max. I'd shake your hand but I'd rather just hold on to my beer." This guy was a character and it'd be fun to get to hang out with Katelyn and her housemates, at least at a later time. But right now all I wanted was to be alone with my girl.

Katelyn squeezed my hand with a slight yank of the arm as if to say, *let's go upstairs* and so I shrugged at Max and we took the steps two at a time.

"He's funny. Is that the one who has a crush on you?" I had to ask.

"Max? God no! I mean I love him, but he's never shown any interest in me." I couldn't help but stare like a pervert at her shapely backside as she led the way up. "Katy will be working at the call centre, so I'll introduce you to her tomorrow." *Tomorrow,* hmmm – I loved how direct she was. I'd be staying the night – With Katelyn – In her bed. Was it ok to burst yet?

We arrived on the landing and headed toward the door at the far end. Then the door which was now behind us opened. "Katelyn?" Came a voice. Bloody hell, any more distractions? This was killing me.

"Hi, Connor." Katelyn said, turning around and gesturing to me. "You ok? This is Jess."

I followed her lead, more out of politeness at this stage rather than from any genuine burning desire to stall any longer. "Hi, pleased to meet you."

"Hi." Connor, every bit the stereotypical image of the surfer dude with his long blond locks and tall, muscular physique oozed confidence and sex appeal as he stepped forward to shake my hand. Damn, but was *this* the guy who had a crush on Katelyn? She'd have to be real gay not to be tempted. "Nice to meet you too. You're the girl who saved Katelyn's life, right?"

Whoa, what had Katelyn been saying? I glanced at her and her eyes flicked away. "Well I wouldn't say that exactly. In fact the more I think about it, the more I think it was Katelyn who saved *my* life."

He crossed his muscular arms and raised an eyebrow. "Really? How exactly?"

Oh, only because she's shown me the true meaning of sharing, of forgiveness, of friendship, of letting go, of lust and quite probably love too. "Because it takes two to share bodily warmth and lift each other's spirits when things are really bad."

"Huh...whoa, I think I'd like to hear more about that, especially the part about sharing bodily warmth." He looked back to my crush. "I heard you broke up with James. I'm just checking you're ok?"

Katelyn smiled and then I felt her squeeze my hand. "I've never been happier."

KATELYN CLOSED THE DOOR BEHIND US AND SILENTLY APPLIED the lock. I would not be escaping this night.

"Oh my God, Katelyn, he's gorgeous! And you're not just a tiny bit tempted?"

She pinned me against the wall with such sudden and unexpected force as to answer the question and then her lips were an inch from mine. "It's only *you* I'm interested in." Her hands moved to my breasts, their fullness filling her hands through the thin layer of dress fabric. "Besides, I think it's just the thought of me with another girl that does it for him." Her hot breath was on my neck. "But he's not ever being a part of this. I'm keeping you all for myself." Her voice dropped a pitch, almost like she'd gone into full animalistic seduction mode.

My wider periphery vision subconsciously surveyed small details from her room; the volleyball trophies, the athletics trophies, her training gear hung up at various spots.

"You like Jennifer Kessy? She is stunningly beautiful!" I nodded to one of several posters of my volleyball idol on the wall, a woman I'd modelled my style of play as well as my hair on.

"Yeah, she's all right." Katelyn ran her hand up the inside of my thigh, squeezing my flesh with a hunger before, through my underwear, she glanced my pussy with the backs of her fingers. "You are soaking wet."

I pulled her lips into mine. The kissing was hard, passionate, almost too much so, but not quite. You can learn a lot from a person's kiss, like how much they respected you, how much they wanted you and whether or not a person loved you. This kiss definitely told me that Katelyn *wanted* me and I knew she was getting the same signals from me as our tongues clashed.

But then Katelyn eased up and backed away, her arms extending as they clung to my breasts before detaching to light several candles spread about the room.

I turned out the light and was greeted by a serene glow – Perfect. "You, Katelyn, so premeditated bringing me back tonight."

She peeled off her t-shirt and tossed it over her shoulder,

exposing her black bra and I gazed hopelessly into her deep cleavage.

"There was no way I was returning home without you." She stepped closer and lightly stroked my arms with the outsides of her fingers, and I shivered from it. I had no idea I was even sensitive in an area like that. She leaned in, kissed me once on the lips, before returning to the other side of the room. Again, I stared longingly at her buttocks as they filled out her jeans, baggy as they were. How did she do it?

She turned on her iPod and lightly swung her hips as Nina Simone came on through the speakers. She was teasing me all right, and she was good at it, the little minx, as if I wasn't wet enough already and I fixated on the king sized bed with a longing and a throbbing ache deep inside my pussy.

She swaggered around and watched me with a sly smile from too far away, unfastened the top button of her jeans and slid down the zipper. She knew how to prolong my suffering and I made a mental note to seek revenge at a later date. Then she turned away again, evidently having just wanted to witness my frustration and then she began slowly tugging off her jeans as she moved down into a crouch. It was my first glimpse of her black lace underwear in too long and whilst holding onto her desk, she slowly straightened her legs as her body remained doubled over. It was all done in time with the music as she shimmied and swayed and I was mesmerised by her long, sculpted legs that led to an ass that was somehow even more perfect. She straightened and moved toward me, my heart thumping hard and with a hand she removed one strap from my halter dress and then the other and I shivered as the material swept down my body and collapsed to the floor.

And then we both stood facing each other, only in our

underwear, and as well as the heated passion of before there was now something else. Now there also existed an even more satisfying logical passion. Because as we stood before each other, naked and vulnerable, I knew we were not merely committing our bodies but also our hearts and our souls. We both wanted this and as we gazed into each other's eyes, there existed a mutual understanding, a love and desire we both shared.

"I'm falling in love with you, Katelyn."

She wiped a tear from my cheek with her thumb and held me close. "I know, I feel the exact same. I think I'm falling head over heels in love with you."

That's what I wanted to hear more than anything else in the world and it would be a moment I'd cherish forever. There was no reason to wait any longer and so I moved my hands around her back as she instinctively did the same and in unison we unhooked each other's bras. I stepped back and we allowed them to fall to the floor. Her breasts barely moved from the loss of support and I gazed down on them with a hunger, craving them, her beautiful globes noticeably larger and fuller than my own.

Our hands found their way to each other's hips, seizing them, our breathing matched for pace and rhythm as we danced a little to the sweet music.

"Ready?" She asked.

"Ready." I whispered back.

Together, our thumbs slipped inside the hem of the other's underwear and I slowly slid the black lace down her thighs as I moved down into a crouch. She did the same as my own black lace underwear were pulled down my legs.

"Looks like *you* were planning on coming back with *me* tonight." Katelyn said, lightly caressing my shaved pussy as we stood and she was holding my underwear which she now pressed to her mouth, inhaling. "Hmm, I could get used to this scent."

I also held Katelyn's underwear, which I planned on taking home. "I plead guilty to that."

If I had any doubts about how Katelyn felt about me, they disappeared as soon as I saw the glistening, moist folds of her vagina. "Looks like I've changed you." She said, running her fingers up and down my sides.

It was true, she had, but I wanted to know her thoughts. "How so?"

"You're no longer so shy being naked around me, are you?"

I laughed and pulled her close, our juices blending around our damp folds. "Katelyn, I think you've turned me inside out. You're such a bad influence."

She wrapped her arms around my waist and effortlessly lifted me from the ground before tossing me to the bed. She almost came down with me but then returned to her feet and surveyed my form from above as I lay supine, my legs spread and tempting. Her breath caught as she stared at my opening, her wicked grin saying everything. "You're definitely not so shy anymore, babe."

I held out my hand, which she took and I pulled her down on top of me. She ran a hand through my hair and then our lips met, filling my world with lavender. I twisted clumps of her hair around in my fingers and lightly stroked the small of her back with my free hand. Our breasts crushed together and Katelyn thrust her hips hard against my own. Our kisses increased in speed and intensity and I felt her hand slowly run down my chest, to my stomach and onto my pubis where she tickled me, teased me. I realised this would be the first time I would ever have been touched on my most intimate of parts and I willed her hand to continue moving south. My breathing increased in depth as her fingers grazed my flesh, sending shivers through my body, her eyes locked on mine. Then she lightly pressed her fingertips against my clit as my body quivered, her fingers moving around so easily due to the slickness.

"I can see you like this, honey." She whispered before adding her kisses to my neck, the sensitive area sending shockwaves around my body. Then she adjusted her angle and her fingers slipped inside me, a million nerve endings telling me I'd been entered. Then I felt her fingers curl as they rubbed against my upper wall.

She gave me one final, soft and passionate kiss on the lips before kissing her way down my body. I was sad to see her go but so happy to know her intentions and as her kisses ventured lower, her fingers gained a better angle and I felt their fullness as they delved deeper inside my pussy.

I released an involuntary moan that came from somewhere deep inside and then her lips were near my clit and I held my breath in anticipation. Katelyn's legs were off the bed now, giving her a better position to enter me further as she...

"Ummm." It came from deep down inside as I felt her tongue slide over my clit for the first time and my lower back arched off the bed.

"Oh, honey...that taste." The second skim of Katelyn's tongue was around my outer lips, scooping up my errant juices. I knew this because it was exactly what I'd imagined doing to her. Then I felt a sudden moist warmth as her mouth enveloped my bud and almost immediately she began sucking interspersed with gentle nibbles and hard flicks with her tongue.

I reeled from the sensations, my back arching ever more and

I reached back for the bedpost and grabbed on for dear life as my knuckles turned white.

Her fingers continued working away, deep inside me, pressing hard against my inner walls.

Katelyn hummed and I felt the vibration on my nerve endings, sending extra shockwaves from my toes to my fingertips. The top of her head bobbed up and down in a slow rhythm as she went to work devouring me.

I felt something brewing from deep within, my body continued to tremble as Katelyn and I experienced this most intimate of moments together.

"Don't stop...don't stop." I panted, almost with a whimper as a firestorm built inside, my back arched to some obscene angle, my breathing increased in intensity and perspiration covered my entire body.

Katelyn increased her speed, curling the tips of her fingers as she rubbed my insides. She sucked harder on my bud, pressing firmly with her tongue.

And then I exploded as I reached down with a hand toward Katelyn, she grabbed it with her free hand and we squeezed hard; we were there together, experiencing this orgasm as one. I felt my juices gushing out from my insides and Katelyn's tongue as she drank every last drop.

She withdrew her fingers and gave a final kiss to my pussy before crawling back up next to me on the bed where I lay shaking and gasping for breath. I was so happy to have her next to me again and without saying a word she wrapped her arms around me, her face next to mine. We gazed into each other's eyes, a look of tenderness in hers, doubtless one of sheer animalistic lust in my own.

"I cannot even begin..." I gasped, trying to regain my

composure. "How...How?"

She stroked my hair and kissed me softly on the lips. "That was for you only."

I held her closer and ran my hand through her hair. I needed to experience her, just as she had me. I needed to see her, to smell her and to taste her. I needed to be inside her, to touch her soul with my own.

I grabbed her arm with a sudden force and levered Katelyn onto her back. I then locked my hands around her wrists as I mounted her and loomed down so my breasts hovered over her eyes. I watched with pleasure as her eyes devoured them, my nipples hard and erect and so sensitive.

"Rough hey? This is a side of you I could get used to and..." her voice trailed off because I'd commenced grinding my pussy against hers, our juices mingling together as one. She shuddered once, and then again but with more ferocity.

"You've been torturing me for longer than you even know, so now I'm finally having my way with you." I had no idea I was even capable of such filth, but I loved it and I certainly couldn't help it. The girl drove me insane. And she certainly didn't appear shocked by my revelation, indeed her eyes remained transfixed on my breasts. It was enough to make me believe she'd planned this, to have me in her bed, for a long time. So be it.

And I'd been neglecting her breasts for too long. Her incredible, large and perfectly round, supple globes with their erect nipples begged for me. Even as she lay there, they were perfect. They'd flattened out at least a little but still kept their fullness. "I fucking love your breasts." I almost stuttered as I finally seized them and they more than filled my hands as I pressed and moulded them to my design.

"I can see that, honey." She closed her eyes and reached behind for the bedposts.

I watched with fascination as her breasts heaved with her ever increasing breaths. Then I lowered myself onto her and cupped her sphere where it met her ribcage, bringing her nipple to my hungry mouth. I felt her body shudder beneath my own as I flicked my tongue repeatedly over her nipple, my free hand continuing to squeeze her other tender breast.

She enjoyed it as much as I did, her deep hums confirming it over and over. Then I began meandering warm kisses down her abdomen, the shape of her abdominal muscles faintly visible. She giggled as I swirled my tongue inside her belly button and then I reached up with a hand which she grabbed and squeezed.

I ran my kisses down her smooth pubic area, the raw smell of Katelyn's essence building the further down I ventured. And then I let go of her hand as my legs ran off the end of the bed, presenting me with the perfect, close up view of her most intimate of parts. Her clit was engorged and begged for my tongue whilst her lips gleamed with the kind of moisture only raw sexual lust could bring. She was ready.

I made myself comfortable and took one final look at her beauty and inhaled the scent. This was it. There was no going back now; after this, I would forever be a changed woman.

I glided the tip of my tongue once over her, from the bottom to the top of her vagina. Her hips thrust up from the bed before settling down again, a sharp cry forced itself from her mouth. I retracted my tongue and spread her moisture over my lips, my taste buds came alive with her juices. Then I lightly teased my tongue over her clit, seeing her bud up close and how enlarged it was. I began gently stroking her outer walls with a finger that easily slipped around due to her natural lubrication intermingling with my own saliva.

Hungry for her, I enveloped her clit with my mouth and at first, gently sucked her, nibbled her and caressed her with my tongue, the taste beyond all description. I slipped a finger inside her passage and it disappeared as her pussy closed around it. I massaged away, feeling her insides as her breathing increased in depth and volume. She let out an indecipherable murmur as I sucked once harder, before returning to the gentle rhythm of before.

I retracted my finger but only so I could enter her with two and her new tightness swallowed them as I filled her. I continued working away, pulling slowly out and searching tenderly back in. Her breathing increased further, which I took as the signal to increase intensity. I pressed my tongue hard against her folds as I curled my two fingers and pressed hard against her inner wall. Another shudder and the arching of her back signalled something incredible was growing within her, preparing to release itself with its full fury.

She gasped, the sound of bedsprings chiming in a fast rhythm. My head moved up and down to a steady beat and then I felt her fingers in my hair. I reached up with my free hand and took hers which she squeezed with an unforeseen force. "I'm close...I'm close!" She panted as my own excitement grew with hers.

Her hips pressed against my face and I knew she was about to come. I sucked harder, pressed harder, rubbed harder and she held her breath, went silent – The calm before the storm – And then the juices gushed from her to flow down the back of my hand. I lowered my lips to collect her essence, not wanting to waste a single drop, her nectar was inside me now and our souls would forever be entwined.

I gave a final kiss to her before clambering back to her side. I hated to leave her but was so happy to be back. We embraced each other and she shivered, her skin noticeably cooler than before, her blood having concentrated lower down for a long time.

We remained silent for several minutes, just gazing into each other. There was nothing that needed to be said, we both understood exactly what had just happened, and what was continuing to happen between us. We were in love and that excited me more than anything else I'd ever experienced.

EPILOGUE

I didn't know when we fell asleep, but soon after we had mind blowing sex we drifted off in each other's arms, just as we'd done many times in Italy. Only now, we'd done so in England, at home and under our own free volition.

It was official – I was a lesbian and I'd never been so happy.

Katelyn stirred, she looked so pretty even in the morning. "Hi." She whispered and I inhaled the scent from the crook of her neck. Her breasts touched my own and was probably the reason, along with her complete proximity, why my pussy was throbbing. I wanted her again and soon.

"Good morning." I replied.

"You have a perverted look on your face."

"I know and I can't help it."

She kissed me, soft and passionately then stood and walked toward the wardrobe. "I'm kind of still finding my *look*." She brought out a few things. "But I don't think I have any real desire to, you know, look gay." She turned her head to look at me, all I could do was stare back in amazement at the naked Katelyn, her body, mine. "I mean, now that I've turned you inside out, do you feel the need to change your style?"

I giggled, I couldn't help it. "I've really not put much thought into it. I don't think so."

"Good, because you really don't need to. You're perfect just the way you are."

And as she began rummaging through her clothes and I ogled her immaculate frame, I realised things really were perfect. Or almost.

There was just one thing that still played on my mind, one small, or rather one large doubt that I needed resolving.

And just as Katelyn had often done in the past, she read my thoughts. "I know what you're thinking, Jess. I'm thinking the exact same thing. We need to have *that* conversation."

"Yes, we do." I said, sitting up in bed, a little terrified.

"Hey, don't look so glum." She bounded over and wrapped her arms around my shoulders, kissing my lips. "I want the exact same things as you do." She pulled away. "But...we have training in one hour."

"Ah, about that." I sucked in air. "I'm still not too sure that..."

"...Jessica, you never gave up on me when we were trapped, not once, not even for a minute. I hope you're not giving up on me now?"

I had to hand it to her. She had a way of making me see clarity. And emotional blackmail worked as well as any other method.

We arrived at training together. Nobody asked any delicate questions, it was just assumed we'd become great friends after our ordeal. There was no need yet to announce to the whole team that Katelyn and I were sleeping together - Oh, how just thinking those thoughts sent me lightheaded.

As expected, I spent the first part of the training session on the bench and watched enthralled as Katelyn smashed point after easy point. Dorothy had put one of the new girls in as middle blocker to replace Amanda, who'd ditched us in favour of her new Italian boyfriend. But after the first game, Dorothy sprang to life and signalled for the new girl to take a rest and guess who was chosen to come on in her place?

Katelyn gave a wry smile as she looked at me from the other side of the court. My God, but I was facing her.

And then the ball was bumped toward her. She jumped and spiked the ball with such extreme force that even I was surprised as the thunderbolt hurtled toward me. At least I now knew how her other victims felt, but then something funny happened. I swear it wasn't intentional but a mere reflex, and as I reached out the ball ricocheted off my arm, hurting no small amount but taking the sting out from the strike. It all happened in slow motion as Marie reacted and leaped up to spike it.

The ball slammed into the net. "Shit!" Marie shouted, holding out an apologetic hand. "Sorry hon, I wasn't expecting you to get that one."

The cheeky cow, I'll show her. "Well could you be prepared next time?"

The next time Katelyn sent the ball shooting toward me I managed to block it with a greater level of control, sending the ball up easily for Marie to spike, which she did, firing a bullet into the far corner of the court.

I didn't notice at the time, such was my concentration, but Dorothy was taking notes and Katelyn was getting flustered.

After the session, I undressed next to my lover and we entered the shower together.

I slapped her bare arse cheek. "I want you to promise that you weren't going easy on me out there."

"I wasn't." She said defensively.

I grabbed her wrist. "Promise?"

"I absolutely promise. Jess, you played a blinder!"

A couple days later I was surprised to receive a call from Dorothy who said I'd be coming on during the second or third game as middle blocker against Worthing VC. I told Katelyn the news immediately and that evening we celebrated with a champagne meal in her room.

The crucial rescheduled match was to be played a few days later and it was in front of Allison Burbridge when, after an hour of play, both teams were tied one game each. I'd been watching from the sidelines rocking back and forth on the bleacher until finally, Dorothy bit the bullet and brought me on.

Katelyn beamed as I trundled on court, my heart beating rapidly, my clammy paws threatening to show me up and cost us the title, and Katelyn a place on the national team. This time I'd be playing *with* her, no pressure, Jess.

Worthing VC scored a few early points, but once I settled down and successfully blocked my first ball, things went a whole lot better. Watching Katelyn destroy them from such close proximity was incredible.

We won the match and went top of the league and later I saw Burbridge conversing with Dorothy, too far away for my prying ears, before she waved to the team and left.

That night I arrived at Katelyn's with a night bag and had to bite my lip to hide the grin.

She locked the door after me and asked immediately. "Well?"

"Well what?" I asked, with mock confusion.

She stamped her foot. "Don't play the goat with me. What did Dorothy say?"

I waved a dismissive hand and, unable to keep it in any longer, feigned placidity. "Oh, only that I need to continue as I was and that Burbridge is interested in my progress." The truth was I still felt uncomfortable in the new position and that I needed more practice to become accustomed there. Thankfully I had the perfect training partner for such things. "But I'm to start against Wessex next week."

She couldn't contain herself and was quick to embrace me before we kissed passionately for several minutes.

Finally, I pulled away and returned the question to her. "And? What did she say to you?"

Her eyes sparkled. "I'm to train with the national team at the next gathering."

My mouth opened wide and I threw my arms around her. "I'm so happy for you, Katelyn."

She grabbed ahold of me, picked me up and dumped me on the bed, falling on top of me. "As it turns out, you just happen to be the best blocker I've ever seen and I'll need you as a partner, now more than ever." Her scent filled my world and I inhaled her deeply.

I kissed her ear. "Sure, I'd be more than happy to be your training partner. It'll work out for us both."

"It will! But I wasn't just talking about *training* partners." She grinned and I doubted she'd ever looked more beautiful.

My heart leapt. "I...you...you mean..." I stuttered but the words wouldn't come.

She giggled. "Jess, I love you more than anything else in the world. I want things to be just like this forever."

"Me too."

"Will you be my girlfriend?" She asked.

The answer was so obvious. "Of course I will."

I pressed my lips against hers and we kissed until the light turned dark.

We didn't emerge until morning.

ALSO BY SALLY BRYAN

Novels

Euro Tripped

Where Are You

A Petal And A Thorn

Novellas

My Summer Romance

Made in the USA
Columbia, SC
25 February 2019